THE INDIVISIBLE
HEART

Visit us at www.boldstrokesbooks.com

THE INDIVISIBLE HEART

by

Patrick Roscoe

A Division of Bold Strokes Books

2015

THE INDIVISIBLE HEART

ISBN 13: 978-1-62639-341-7

This Trade Paperback Original Is Published By
Bold Strokes Books, Inc.
P.O. Box 249
Valley Falls, NY 12185

First Edition: April 2015

CREDITS
EDITOR: JERRY WHEELER
PRODUCTION DESIGN: STACIA SEAMAN
FRONT COVER IMAGE: "PATRICK ROSCOE IN THE LABORATORY OF LOVE"
   © OLIVIER DE MADERAS
COVER DESIGN BY SHERI (GRAPHICARTIST2020@HOTMAIL.COM)

This book is for all those who cut its design into my flesh with their knowing knives.

PART ONE

Again I've been sent out into the demanding night to find what you need. I know what this is because once it was me. That boy of twenty years ago, myself at sixteen, is who you require still. It isn't a question of providing you with an exact replica of how I appeared then. An offering's features and form needn't duplicate mine. What matters is the smoothness of his unlined skin, the texture of taut flesh. Clear eyes and eager mouth; petal lips, pristine penis. As the intangible attributes of a wing can be known only to the bird, I alone am equipped to recognize with authority the collection of qualities which will soar you to satisfaction. The feathers that will fan your flames. Although your physical gifts allow you to swoop down and capture the wariest prey with ease, we discovered at the beginning that the urgency of your need blunts the precise aim necessary for its fulfillment. Several disappointing incidents taught us that I'm better positioned to perform this essential task, being one step removed from your longing but one step closer to its original source. I never fail because my survival depends on pleasing you. I'm useful to you only as long as I can bring you what you want.

❖

The nude body found face down on the bed is that of a white male. He is six feet tall and likely weighs one hundred and seventy-five pounds. Initial observation suggests he is approximately thirty-five years old. The musculature is pronounced and defined, indicating a general state of excellent health prior to death.

❖

I find tonight's beautiful boy easily. Fifteen years have perfected my procedure, honed my skill at applying it. For the past three months in this southern European city, while your desire has once again waxed according to a schedule as fixed as the phases of the moon, I've scouted where the most likely possibilities to satisfy you loiter. Beside the river that divides the city in two, at the mouth of the dark tunnel running beneath a bridge. Members of a rowing club linger on the embankment there after they finish stroking the water below at evening.

I always make a point of observing, during our gym workouts at each site of operations, whether you gaze at blond rather than dark-haired boys; to ones tall and lean; or to those shorter and more heavily muscled. Sometimes you want a shy boy, or you might delight in a bold one instead.

My function is to provide your need of the moment without having to ask what special qualities will meet it. It's critical to prepare at leisure, while I am able to deliberate and weigh, how I can feed your hunger swiftly when it arises. You won't be able to wait more than a few hours. If I take too long to find you sustenance, I fear you'll be gone when I return with it. Several times at the beginning, when my system of supplying you was imperfect, and I failed to understand the importance of advance reconnaissance, haste made me blunder in choosing a specimen. The consequences of your disappointment were harsh. You were forced to cut and mark my flesh to an unusual extreme.

You've made it clear that if I'm unable to perform my duty, others are. Perhaps this amounted to a bluff, but I haven't been able to call it. *Only the bird knows the wing*, I assure myself again. In a dark chamber far beneath my skin huddles the truth about our love: I'm as expendable as the offerings I bring to you.

❖

The back surface of the body is covered with scars that appear unlikely to have been left by a dermatological condition. The possibility will be ruled out by the medical examiner immediately. The profusion and nature of marks— they blanket the skin nearly completely—negates the chance that all of them could have originated in a single serious accident or in a series of minor ones. The autopsy will confirm what seems apparent at initial observation: the victim's skin presents evidence of having sustained numerous deliberately inflicted injuries. The wide range of shades among the scars—some are dark red, some paled to near invisibility— indicates that mutilation occurred at divergent points of time over the course of an extended period, perhaps one as long as several decades.

❖

I barely glance at the boy I'm leading toward where you wait. He's neither more nor less beautiful than any of his sixty predecessors, I suppose. Once satisfied he's what you need, I have no further interest in him. I've nearly forgotten what he looks like already; it would be impossible for me to describe him to the police. I can't remember his name even though I was told it fifteen minutes ago. It requires effort not to recoil when his sleeve brushes mine. I force myself not to shrug off his hand when it rests for a moment on my shoulder. Any touch except yours is distasteful.

❖

Scattered among the scars are a substantial number of wounds. The extent to which each has healed indicates when it was inflicted in the course of recent weeks. The freshest wounds, still bleeding, were obviously received immediately prior to death. Viewed together, the wounds present a timeline of trauma. Another calendar of the crime is provided by the blood on the sheets, which is alternately wet, partly coagulated, and completely dry. This suggests the final violence occurred over a twelve-hour period lasting almost to the moment the victim was discovered. The blood's failure to have pooled to a significant degree anywhere on the bed points to the likelihood the victim was shifted frequently over the course of being assaulted. None of his injuries appear to have been received in attempted self-defence. His hands and forearms remain unharmed. Laboratory analysis will determine that all the blood at crime scene belongs to the victim. According to a preliminary autopsy, none of the recent wounds to the body was fatal in itself or in concert with others. The official cause of death will await the result of a toxicology exam to be performed in Madrid.

❖

The boy beside me chatters from nervous excitement at the prospect of what he thinks awaits him. I provide rote responses designed to allay any second thoughts he might be forming. It's critical that this specimen not be allowed to escape. The time-bomb of your desire ticks; once underway, its countdown can't be halted or paused. I'm careful to avoid correcting the boy's impression that within moments he'll be mine. Mention of you, an unknown element, might frighten him at this point, when he believes it's me he wants.

He doesn't know that while sufficient to snare a boy for you with little effort, my looks are far less dazzling than yours. He's unequipped to understand how the first sight of your beauty will cause him to forget my presence immediately. Like all the others of the past fifteen years, tonight's offering won't even notice me leave a moment after I hand him over to you. Before your fly has been unbuttoned, he'll be breathing quickly. Blood will flush his cheeks, and his mouth will dry as he struggles to swallow. I don't have to linger to know he'll begin to moan when you reveal the length and girth of what you have for him. In timbre and pitch and tone, the sound will be identical to the one that you've been inducing from my throat over the course of twenty years. To objective ears, this boy's moan would be indistinguishable from mine.

As though both were made by the same voice, pushed by a single pair of lungs.

❖

The autopsy will determine that a majority of the fresh wounds and probably a proportionate number of those long healed were made by knives. As many as a dozen varieties were involved: ones meant for the kitchen and for hunting, for cutting and for carving. The blades were of differing length, width, and sharpness. In some instances, the top layer of skin has been sliced shallowly in a criss-cross pattern or etched with a more elusive design. In others, the flesh was profoundly gouged. Nails and bolts and screws, with finer or blunter points, were also driven into the victim to varying depths over the length of his twenty or so years of torture.

The autopsy will find that a lesser number of the scars were caused by burns from directly applied heat or from contact with an assortment of acids and chemical solutions. Signs of multiple abrasions to the neck, wrists, and ankles reveal that the victim was often tightly bound, again at widely divergent points in time, with rope, cord, and, almost certainly but not definitively, wire.

The coroner will emphasize that considerable care had to have been taken to avoid puncturing organs, severing arteries, or otherwise causing fatal harm in the course of assaults prior to the final one. From this finding will arise the premise that the perpetrator has some degree of medical knowledge and/or laboratory experience. In addition, it will be judged highly improbable that the torturer performed his deeds in a state of psychological crisis or emotional disarray; neither under the influence of powerful drugs nor in a frenzy of uncontrollable emotion. Systematic and sustained, the mutilation was a result of careful forethought and deft execution.

❖

As the boy and I move closer to where you wait, I sense your impatience as an audible vibration reaching toward me through the night. The humming contains a note of warning, though the current procedure has so far unfolded without incident and at acceptable speed. Did I choose carefully enough, after all? I used to believe offering you the perfect boy would bury your longing for further ones in a grave too deep to permit resurrection. You experience total satisfaction in youthful flesh, you extract all the pleasure it can afford; you are left needing only me.

Aiming to encounter the ultimate candidate, I'd hesitate a dangerously long time to make my choice. But risking your wrath with delay served no purpose. It became clear that a more beautiful boy leaves you satisfied for no longer afterward than a less beautiful one does. An exact incarnation of myself at sixteen wouldn't be enough. I learned to settle on a boy whose beauty could meet the needs of the moment. At the same time, I accepted that this occasion would occur again and again, without end. Despite my preparations and planning in anticipation of what I'm certain will come, your acute ache for another emerges as a surprise to me each time.

❖

The victim had been repeatedly sodomized in the hours before his death. He was also anally assaulted more than once with objects, perhaps iron bars and wooden implements, which caused extensive damage to the rectum. The large amount of semen found in his throat initially suggests it was deposited by at least several secretors. Analysis of the ejaculate disproves this possibility.

❖

A quick look at the boy walking with me assures that tonight I have again selected correctly. Almost simultaneously, my glance produces a twinge of doubt. Is there something familiar about the face floating beside me? Do I know the contours of his cheekbones and the clean sweep of his brow from before these past months of scouting? Can I have brought him to you once already, long ago, on a previous sojourn in this southern city? Impossible. We leave each site of operations immediately after you finish with the boy offered by it. We never return; there's no reason to. A limitless number of cities offer an inexhaustible supply of fresh material. Without explaining why, you've emphasized that revisiting any place already plundered would be dangerous. If we have come back here despite your rule against a return, the earlier stay surely occurred long enough ago that tonight's specimen would have been far too young to evoke your sexual interest. You frown in seeming annoyance at the sight of little boys in the street. Their shrill voices make you wince. The same high, thin calls produce a subtle kick within my belly. A responsive inner stirring. An answering cry from deep beneath my skin, nearly too faint for me to hear.

❖

Manuel Arroyo, the senior detective in the Sevilla homicide division, arrives at the crime scene within an hour of its discovery. He's forty-eight, divorced, and locally born, with a reputation for being persistent and meticulous on the job. His preference for investigating even complex crimes without leg-work assistance from junior detectives goes against policy. Some feel this is an indication of a possessive, overly personal attitude toward his cases. To date, the detective's desire to work on his own has been allowed, in part, because of the results he achieves this way and, in part, because of a perennial shortage of manpower within the division. Despite his independent streak, Arroyo has a history of welcoming the close involvement of Olivier Joaquin Ortega, one of several forensic psychologists attached to the homicide division in certain cases. He generously grants that the expert's input has been critical in solving a number of them. The detective obviously feels the murder at Caballerizas, 4 will be one of those cases. He calls Olivier Joaquin Ortega less than fifteen minutes after arriving at the address where the crime occurred.

❖

Like your desire, as soon as my uncertainty about tonight's boy appears, it begins to swell, to insist. It demands I realize the frailty of my memory and the obscurity in which I live as a result. Of the present, I am certain only that I'm thirty-six, this city is named Sevilla, the month is now October. My factual knowledge of the past is limited nearly to several dates marking our history: you found me when I was sixteen and you were twenty-one; your need for another boy first arose five years later; that desire has reappeared at three-month intervals ever since. Just as the face of each of those specimens is forgotten as soon as he's secured for you, the landscape to offer him up vanishes with similar swiftness from my mind. I'm unable to recall the cities which have one after the other served as temporary settings for our love. Even their names are lost to me. I couldn't describe the apartments we've rented, the streets surrounding them, or the climate to contain them. Such details are irrelevant. All I require to remember is the taste of your last kiss, and what had to be done in order that the next one could be savoured. Scenery is out-of-focus background against which you pose, weather the unregistered fluctuations of atmosphere you breathe. I haven't room in my mind for more than you. Some day—I believe, I hope, I pray—all voices except yours will become garbled noise; every sight except of you will be one indistinguishable blur; any touch not yours will go unfelt. Eventually, I'll be able to hear only your voice, see just your face, feel nothing except your lips and hands. The world beyond falls into darkness then from existence. In a holy void, alone together, there is only us.

The swift discovery of the body wasn't the consequence of alarm being raised by sounds of violence from the apartment in question. Interviews with residents living adjacent to 2-A, and with those above and below, elicit that they heard no disturbance. Neither did neighbours from

across the courtyard nor from several farther courtyards in the building detect anything out of the ordinary at the time. It's explained to Manuel Arroyo that Caballerizas, 4 is always quiet. The tenants are sober, responsible, respectable. No one without means could afford to live at the address. The historically important building is marked on most tourist maps of Sevilla, indicating a former palace which has been immaculately restored and meticulously maintained at considerable expense. It contains a trio of spacious patios, one leading into another, each with marble floors and frescoed walls, with arches and columns. All are attractively decorated with potted ferns and palms. A fountain occupies the centre of the courtyard nearest the street door through which residents enter and exit the building. One of the city's prominent churches rises adjacently; across the narrow, cobblestoned street stands the Monasterio de San Leandro. Monks can sometimes be glimpsed beyond the gates of the retreat. As they pace, the ends of cords fastened around their waists swing like pendulums trapped in perpetual movement between the forces of left and right, heaven and hell, good and evil.

❖

The humming in the air has become an angry buzz. Though the boy and I continue to walk quickly, I am taking too long to bring him to you. Exploration of various routes between the river and where you wait led me to decide that this one, passing through a trio of major plazas would be the simplest and most time-effective. Because few of this city's streets are laid out in straight lines, and many bend and wind bewilderingly, I practised following my course to avoid any chance of becoming lost when it would matter. There can be no hesitating uncertainly on corners or retracing of mistaken steps while you are throbbing with impatience. Yet these initial blocks have seemed as unfamiliar as the stores lining them. When a plaza appears ahead, it looks different than the one marking my route. Have I blundered off path despite my preparations? Or am I deliberately wandering aimlessly with this boy beside me? Recklessly delaying his deliverance? I steal another glance at his face, as though the answer lies there.

The discovery of the body was made by the widow who for the past twenty of her sixty-two years has lived in the second-floor apartment to the immediate right of 2-A. Walking toward the staircase that leads down to the outermost patio of the building, Raimunda Nuñez Moreno de Guerra noticed the door adjacent to hers was open. It wasn't just ajar, she stresses to Manuel Arroyo. She explains to the detective that out of discretion—that is, from courtesy—residents of Caballerizas, 4 don't leave their apartments open as a rule. You close the door behind you as soon as you go in or go out. The occupants of 2-A had never failed to do so in the three months since moving in, as far as Raimunda had noticed. The two men usually went out just once a day, most often together, in the early afternoon. It was Raimunda's impression that they waited to exit down the stairs and through the courtyards until they would be unseen by coming or going neighbours. She had passed them on their way in several times, but greetings or

pleasantries weren't exchanged on these encounters. "To spare them embarrassment," Raimunda said to explain her side of the silence. "Most of these foreigners don't speak or understand Spanish, do they?" The widow was able to describe the two men only vaguely. She supposed they were both tall, fairly young, decently dressed. The other tenant— not the one whose body she found—might have been blond. Once satisfied these new neighbours would prove acceptably quiet, Raimunda's interest in them ended. "Foreigners," she added, as if Manuel had questioned her lack of curiosity. She looked at him knowingly, one Sevillano to another. "There's more and more of them since '92."

❖

It's not my surroundings that are unfamiliar, I realize, but the way they're encroaching on my senses. Usually the world beyond your arms lies at a remove, as two-dimensional and artificial as painted paper scenery. It lacks depth and texture; the air has no temperature, holds no aromas. Sounds are muted. Passersby might be alien forms of life whose actions require interpretation to be understood. With a distant pity mixed with scorn, I view them scurrying in apparent search of pleasure and comfort and distraction. Lacking a love like ours, they're frantic. Without you, I'd be similarly lost. As disoriented perhaps as I feel now. My confusion must show on my face. The boy's hand touches my shoulder. "It will be all right," he says, as though our roles have become reversed. As though I were the one in need of assurance now.

❖

Raimunda hesitated in the hall outside 2-A for several moments after receiving no response to her repeated calls through the open door. When she finally entered the apartment, it wasn't from a sense that anything might be wrong inside. Her intent was merely to remind her neighbours that in a building where decorum prevails, a door left open is unacceptable.

❖

My confusion is increased by the Spanish tonight's offering chatters in. Whatever country your desire draws us to, I must learn to speak and understand the local language sufficiently to accomplish our purpose there. One of my obligations on our arrival in Prague would be to gain a good grasp of Czech, or with re-familiarizing myself with its rudiments from a forgotten sojourn in another of the country's cities. The vocabulary required to secure an offering for you is as limited in Italian as it is in Danish. I've no interest in listening to or speaking with any specimen beyond that parameter.

I don't wish to hear the one with me now as he describes his pleasure in rowing on the river beside which I found him. The facility with which I understand each of his words prickles my skin; I understand too much slang than can explained by any number of forgotten three-month experiences in any number of disremembered Spanish-speaking cities. The particular accent flavouring the boy's speech insinuates into my ears like an unwanted intimacy, illuminates a vision of the *barrio* where this intonation must flourish. The name of the neighbourhood chimes inside me, like a bell tolling from a subterranean cathedral. *La Macarena*. I've glimpsed that eroding area of the city only in a few pictures in guide books for the city. I'm aware that it lies no more than ten minutes by foot from where the boy and I are walking but exists decades in the past. Details of the place flicker unaccountably in the apses of my mind. On benches, thin-lipped old men with right-wing newspapers spread like napkins over their laps enjoy nostalgic dreams of Franco. Housewives dressed in styles of the 1950s bargain for cows' heads in the markets. Black-draped crones teeter toward unrestored churches. Potted carnations decorate the crumbling balconies. Where have these images come from, and why do they linger to lick my mind? The guide books made it clear that La Macarena wouldn't offer me a useful hunting ground. I've never been there in my life.

❖

Raimunda's first impression of 2-A was that it looked unusually bare. The rooms beyond the entrance hall where she paused lay in dimness; the curtains on the salon windows overlooking the street were presumably closed. The silence surrounding the widow was complete; she could hear her watch. The ticking reminded her that a friend was waiting in the nearby Plaza de la Alfalfa. Raimunda had arranged to meet her for an aperitif outside the Café Realito at six p.m. She glanced at her watch. It was six fifteen. Not wishing to be later than she already was, she walked past a bathroom and kitchen with no more than a glance into them. The apartment was laid out identically to hers. Knowing where the bedroom would be, she walked toward it without calling out. At a three-foot distance from the open door, she could see the body on the bed beyond. It wasn't necessary to approach nearer to realize she had to leave the apartment at once. Raimunda wasn't able to say why she had gone directly to the bedroom rather than to the salon. She did explain to Manuel Arroyo that she remained silent when she saw the body in order to avoid alerting an assailant who might still be somewhere in 2-A. She returned to her apartment and locked the door behind her. After calling her friend's cell to explain she couldn't keep their appointment, Raimunda Nuñez dialled the police.

The voice in my ear detonates further bursts of light in my brain, burns holes in the film separating me and the world that has long lain beyond my interest. The night suddenly possesses the clarity of a hallucination. Distances dissolve with alarming speed. Surroundings with two dimensions grow distorted at acquiring a third and seem to crowd in on me menacingly. The air's warmth and cacophony are overpowering; intense aromas threaten to make me swoon, encourage me to sink to the ground and curl around myself. The presence breathing beside me reminds me of my purpose. I force myself forward into another plaza with him. I command myself in your voice to acknowledge that the place holds no harm. At once, it appears benign. A plaque on a wall assures me I'm not lost: the Plaza de Jesus de la Passion is the second one on my route.

I must have passed through this square dozens of times before, but still it looks puzzlingly altered. Now, after midnight, it is filled with activity that appears relaxed and lively at once. Diners enjoy al fresco meals at tables set at the perimeter of the open space. Elderly couples with ice cream lounge on benches and teens throng with plastic cups of beer before the bars. Everywhere small children play games with balls. When I wonder why such little boys are still up at this late hour, their excited screams prompt a kick inside my belly much more forceful than any induced by the sound before. As though it's also been struck, my head immediately begins to ache in the way it does on mornings after you've given me a stronger than usual dose of your tincture. You hold the glass of cloudy liquid to my lips on nights when I feel anxious despite being safe in your arms. Sometimes thought of one or another souvenir of a boy unaccountably disturbs me in the darkness. An ordinary blue t-shirt, slightly frayed around the neck, with a loose thread at the waist. Unless I drink your bitter draught, my mind will keep fingering the stray thread, though I'm frightened that if I keep worrying it, the whole fabric of our life together will unravel.

❖

No identification documents belonging either to the victim or to the second occupant of 2-A are discovered in the apartment. The rooms fail to offer up receipts, ticket stubs, or notes of any kind. A trace of ash on the floor next to the toilet is determined to be the burned remnants of paper. With two exceptions, all personal effects of the tenants have been removed. The refrigerator is bare. No trash awaits disposal. The buzón pertaining to 2-A is the only one of the mailboxes in the outermost courtyard not labelled with a name or names.

The mailman for the building will state that he delivered no letters or bills to it. The real estate agent for apartment 2-A confirms that it was rented fully furnished and equipped; this includes the sheets now ruined by blood. Consultation of Maria del Carmen Vasquez's detailed inventory of items present upon occupancy reveals that none are missing.

❖

The narrow street leading from the Plaza de Jesus de la Passion gleams like the passage from a childhood dream of searching for the lost home, the missing father. The boy beside me in the shining light is young enough to be my son. As though propelled by a shared vision, he blurts that his father left to live in the Canary Islands five years ago and hasn't been heard from since. The remark unsettles me enough to make me look at tonight's specimen again.

He's fingering a braided multi-coloured band on his left wrist. I can't tell whether the apparently unconscious gesture is out of habit or nervousness. Light catches a small, round medallion, probably with religious significance and perhaps gold, which hangs on a fine chain against a smooth throat. The boy feels the glinting disk several times, as though seeking assurance. His worrying the braided band and touching the gold medallion seem to release an aroma from his body. The scent suggests something dark and cold and clean, in a complex combination with something rich and warm. I shake my head. The scent isn't concentrated in the presence beside me but diffused in the air around me.

Through lamp-lit darkness carry chords from an accordion whose volume points to a source nearby. A street musician must be playing in the shadows, just out of sight. I can't decide whether the tune is plaintive or playful. Every time it seems about to convey one of these qualities definitively, the music breaks off mid-phrase, as though the player has lost interest or is too weak to continue without resting. In each pause before the accordion resumes, the buzzing of your desire sounds louder and angrier, and more insistent that my attention be trained, in equal parts, on you and the boy I'm bringing you. It seems almost surprising that he remains beside me. Due to an accident of time and space, from pure coincidence, the individual journeys of two strangers can for a while appear to be a single one undertaken together. Sooner or later, divergent directions are asserted by separate desires. At a corner, one traveller turns right or left while the other proceeds forward. Neither party makes a sign that an experience shared because of chance has ended. The boy at my shoulder might head his own way at the end of the next block without a word of goodbye. Even the remote possibility of that occurrence should cause me panic. Instead, it seems a matter deserving of more or less the same indifference I feel in regard to whether the accordion tune sounds finally playful or plaintive, whether the instrument's tone is rich or thin. What does seem significant about the music is that it reaches with undiminished volume and clarity despite my forward movement. The accordion player is maintaining the same distance from me, either in front or behind, by strolling approximately at my pace. And at the pace of the boy beside me, I think almost as an afterthought.

❖

Only several articles extraneous to the real estate agent's inventory list are present in 2-A. The first is an athletic bag manufactured and widely available in France but not sold in Spain. It contains a single outfit of clothing and one pair of shoes, fairly new and expensive, which are believed at first to be what the victim was wearing when he undressed, or was undressed, prior to death. Later, both clothes and shoes are ruled out, because of their too-large size, as unlikely to have belonged to the victim. DNA tests back up this theory. Laboratory analysis confirms that particles of hair and skin on the clothes and shoes also don't match those, presumably of the assailant, found in the sheets and on the tiled floor around the bed either. Surfaces beyond the immediate crime site had been thoroughly scoured with common household cleaning products. No usable fingerprints are found on the victim, the bed, or elsewhere in the apartment. The second item not included in 2-A's inventory, and which Maria del Carmen Velasquez testifies having never seen before, is a knife lying in plain view on the sheets beside the body. Its eight-inch serrated blade matches several, but not all of the freshest wounds. Both handle and blade were wiped clean after the knife's use. Olivier Joaquin Ortega comes to believe that, viewed in context of an otherwise carefully staged crime scene, the existence of the knife betrays a murderer's conflicting wishes to elude and to abet capture. It points to a certain arrogance or indifference, which might both, suggests Ortega, be manifestations of the same impulse. The pathologist thinks it doubtful the weapon was left on the bed by accident.

❖

The boy is clinging like a shadow I couldn't shake if I wanted to. Were I to slip suddenly into a dark doorway or around a corner, he'd still be with me. The unwanted illumination cast by his presence would remain. The street leading toward a third plaza shines from the sluicing this city receives each midnight. Cleaning crews in uniforms of orange are winding up long hoses on the corners. Darkened patches of footprints reveal where people have walked since the watering. Upon the cobblestones glow offerings of lamps encased in hexagons of wrought-iron glass attached at intervals to the stone walls on either side. The glass softens and colours the lights. Each pool of gold at my feet seems to lead not forward but back. Not toward you but away.

❖

Maria del Carmen Velasquez is unable to produce the lease for the apartment where the murder occurred but attests that it was negotiated and signed by the tenant whose whereabouts are currently unknown. She didn't meet or hear mention of the victim at that point, nor become subsequently aware of a second tenant in 2-A. It was her understanding all along that this was a single-occupancy situation. She has no record of passport information pertaining to the client with whom she did deal, but states he produced the document as required by law. She believes the passport was issued by Switzerland. While unable to remember a first or last name or to suggest ones to sound like them, neither seemed especially Swiss to her. She doesn't think the man was European, though she can't say why.

"He was extremely handsome," she repeats three times

to Manuel during the course of this brief initial interview. Negotiations for the lease were concluded swiftly in English, despite the real estate agent's admitted weakness with the language. That limitation prevents her from hazarding whether the client might have had a British or American accent. She sensed he could speak only a few words of Spanish. Carmen, as the real estate agent preferred to be called, apologizes to Manuel Arroyo for her failure to be more helpful regarding these points.

She explains that her agency is overwhelmed by the city's thriving real estate market, and blames the matter of the missing lease on an assistant whose carelessness with filing was one reason among several for her recent dismissal. While the Caballerizas listing was and is an excellent one, the real estate agent further explains, demands of much more significant properties on her attention would normally have required it be handled by that assistant. The apartment was personally shown by Carmen because of its convenient location, just a block's distance from her Calle Boteros agency, and because she sensed the client was highly motivated. Her instinct proved correct. A standard one-year lease for 2-A was signed less than an hour after it was seen. A cash payment of forty-two thousand euros— representing three months of rent, plus the equivalent of two months as a security deposit and one month for agency fees—compensated for the client's reluctance to provide personal, financial, and employer references.

Though seeming less impressed than perhaps he should have been by the apartment or the building, the client didn't ask to be shown others. His only question during the viewing regarded the degree of privacy afforded by an open courtyard design and to whether this would result in a possibility of suffering disturbance by the noise of neighbours. As for the fired assistant, Carmen couldn't help Manuel Arroyo in locating her. The employee had apparently removed all her personal information from the agency files when she left. Many vital business papers were taken as well. Carmen had suspected this assistant from the start. It wouldn't surprise her if the girl was aiming to set up her own agency with a list of poached clients who had been nurtured by Carmen with patience and care.

❖

The third and final square along the route that leads to you is emptier and quieter than the previous ones. It also appears more familiar. The bars and cafés of the Plaza de la Alfalfa are dark. A flower and a newspaper kiosk are both closed. Only a few youths linger with *galenas* of beer beneath the plane trees. To the left of where the boy and I pass, a low fence of plastic slats encloses a small playground with several swings and ladders and tunnels. My step slows then stops, as though a gang of ghostly children are calling for me to stay with them. They want my company or need my protection. The invitation invokes another disturbance in the pit of my stomach. Through the eyes of a lone starling still awake in one of the plane trees high above, I look down at two figures paused beneath a lamp below.

They're standing as close together as lovers. From my perspective, they might be twins. As though made dizzy by the sensation of unaccustomed flight, my heart drops into my throat when I swoop down toward the pair. Darkness rushes, then clears. I'm standing back on my own two feet beside a boy. My shoulders tremble from the effort of having used long neglected wings. The plane leaves spread silent and still overhead. I look into the eyes of the boy before me; they hold both questions and answers. They tell me I know his name. Jose Manuel. They tell me that each plaza of tonight's journey in his company has presented a more intense vision of a similar atmosphere, or allowed its essence to be entered more deeply than that of the one before. Traversing the three squares has been more than a forward movement through time and space. It's been a progression in understanding that promises to lead toward a revelation I haven't anticipated and don't desire.

❖

The victim presents the most important evidence at the crime scene. The front of his body, especially the abdomen and chest, shows it had been mutilated as severely and over as long a period of time as the back. Extra brutality was inflicted on the genitalia. Unlike its posterior, the front surface of the body bore no wounds sufficiently recent to have been bleeding at the time of death. Manuel had a hunch this would prove to be true before the victim was turned over.

It is the unmarked condition of his face that surprises the detective. His first in-depth discussion of the case with Olivier Ortega focuses on this detail. Not only was the face left unscathed, it had been painstakingly tended with a sophisticated regimen of lotions and creams, cleansers and toners and exfoliants, anti-wrinkle agents and anti-

aging serums, according to the dermatologist brought in for consultation on this point. As a result of such care, the victim's face would have had an appearance of being perhaps five years younger than his approximated age of thirty-five.

Olivier Ortega believes it must have been important to the inflictor of the torture that his victim be able to go out in public between each incident. An absence of old scars as well as recent wounds on the hands supports this theory. Wearing long sleeves and trousers, he would not attract negative attention. On the contrary, his appearance seemed designed to allure. The victim's impressive physique had obviously been built by a program of exercise as exacting as the one devoted to his face. His hair was expensively cut. Interviews conducted by Manuel with witnesses of the victim have invariably included a mention of him being attractively dressed.

Presumably, the perpetrator received as much satisfaction from the act of parading his victim in public as from the torture itself. Perhaps his compulsion was, in part, to mock society's superficial powers of observation; its vulnerability to being easily deceived by a pleasing visible surface. Staring at the wall of Manuel's office, where this meeting takes place, Ortega pauses. The detective waits. He's accustomed to his colleague's behavioural quirks, which include a tendency to avoid eye-contact, and which prompt joking within the division that it takes a strange one to understand aberrance in others. These comments are encouraged by the privacy—some would say secrecy—maintained by Ortega about his personal life.

Little is known of the man away from the job except

that he lives, presumably alone, in an apartment on Menendez Pelayo. He avoids socializing with detectives or other colleagues. His contract with the homicide division allows him to travel frequently throughout Spain and within Europe to present lectures and attend conferences related to his field of expertise. He might as well be in Paris right now, Manuel thinks just before the silent man glances at him then quickly looks away again and speaks. If the perpetrator's pathology was expressed by the need to mutilate a single victim numerous times over the course of an extended period, suggests Ortega, it must have been essential that his subject be not only publicly presentable between each incident but seductive in appearance for that torture to continue.

I walk the final blocks toward you still more quickly, as if running away from rather than leading the boy behind me. He and I enter the labyrinth that forms the oldest and best preserved area of the city. Both the twisting streets and the sidewalks are so narrow that pedestrians must press against the walls for a car to squeeze past. My pace slows on reaching an immense church that looms in darkness beyond a locked iron gate. I pause before the adjacent building. With one of two large keys, I open a heavy wooden door studded with brass, then feel on the wall to my right for a switch that illuminates the darkness inside. The light makes a loud buzzing that overwhelms the sound of your desire. Without your signal to guide me, I'm lost.

I blink at a seemingly unfamiliar marble patio that contains palms and ferns, with a still fountain in the centre.

Three storeys of surrounding apartments lay dark. Through an arch beckons another patio; beyond that waits a third. As I wonder whether my key has opened the door of the wrong building, the boy at my shoulder whistles softly. The sound touches a spring in my mind and releases memory. For three months, this place has housed the centre of an operation coming to fruition tonight.

Entering or exiting in daytime has usually meant passing through a gaggle of tourists pointing cameras at our building or at the facing monastery, the adjacent church. The possibility of your image being captured on film, even accidentally and innocuously, makes you wary. A visual record of our presence, here or anywhere, might be used against us in some way. In spite of the undesirable attention drawn by the aesthetic beauty and historical importance of the building, you were attracted to its thick stone walls, its extremely high apartment ceilings, and the heavy wooden shutters over double-paned windows. Noise of neighbours beside or below us has been rarely audible, as only the faintest muffle. Loud sounds occurring in our rooms would go equally unheard by them. For example: shrieking, screaming, cries for help.

❖

Besides insight into the possible psychological circumstances that culminated in his death, the unmarked condition of the victim's face offered a tool that might help solve his murder. Manuel was able to use a photo taken at the crime scene in his investigation. In his experience, it was rare that a face frozen at the moment of violent death, even one unscathed, can be identified by witnesses who have seen it just several times and at some distance in life. The post-mortem expression is almost always too severely distorted. Features appear twisted by terror and realigned by agony into a grotesque mask that bears scant resemblance to any face that might have been glimpsed in the ordinary world. In the absence of other photographs of the victim, and of any of the second occupant of 2-A, it was fortuitous for Manuel's purposes that the crime scene image of the former afforded an exception. The victim's face appeared natural. It showed no sign of pain or fear.

On being shown a copy of the victim photo, Olivier Ortega seemed about to speak, then paused. "A good image," he said a moment later.

Manuel felt that the pathologist had censored his immediate response to the photo. He looks happy, *Manuel believed the man wanted to say.*

❖

A marble staircase in the third courtyard leads to the first-floor apartment where you wait. The boy behind me must be synchronizing his steps to mine. He must be holding his breath. I can't hear him; I might be making this ascent alone. Before opening our door with the second large key, I mention that a friend might be at home. It takes the lightest touch to nudge the boy inside, as though he were a ghost. The ajar door reveals an apparently unoccupied space dimly lit by several lamps and candles beyond. You must be waiting in the bedroom. You must be caressing the implements that in a moment you'll begin to use. For the first time, I don't follow my gift inside to make a quick introduction before leaving. I can't bear to glimpse this offering's eyes widen at the sight of you. To see your gaze fixed on what I've delivered to you tonight. To be reminded that your focus can exclude me entirely. To know that now I don't exist for you, while for me you are always everything, always all.

❖

The post-mortem image of the victim's face accompanied a twelve-line report of the murder that appeared four days afterwards among the pages of local news in the Andalucía edition of El Pais. *The abbreviated nature of the story was determined by the limited information provided to the newspaper's crime reporter. Location: Caballerizas, 4. Victim: unidentified foreigner. Presumed but not yet official cause of death: multiple stab wounds. Prime suspect: second resident of address, unidentified foreigner, whereabouts unknown. Investigation: ongoing.*

The article concluded by stating that the crime was believed to be a homosexual one. This detail had not been given to the reporter, though since his earliest discussions with Ortega, Manuel Arroyo had been pursuing the investigation on the basis of that theory. On the afternoon of the article's publication, the detective received a telephone call from Maria Carmen del Vasquez to complain that surely it was unnecessary to identify an apartment she would have to rent in the future as having been the location of an unsavoury crime. Two days later, the letters to the newspaper's editor included a reprimand from the local chapter of Spain's National Association for the Protection

of Gays, Lesbians, Bisexuals, and Transgendered Citizens.
How can the act of murder be "homosexual" any more than
it can be "heterosexual," regardless who commits and who
suffers it? It would have been hoped that the reporter for a
respected newspaper might write with greater care to avoid
causing offence and possible harm to a large segment of
readers through this kind of imprecise use of language.

The timed light in the patios below switches off. The
loud buzzing stops. I'm surrounded by pitch darkness and
pure silence. I can't knock on our closed door and ask you
to re-activate the light with the button situated just inside.
You're otherwise engaged already. I feel my way down
stairs and cross three patios without blundering into the
fountain in the final one. As I reach for the door to the street,
a light goes on and then off in the ground-floor apartment to
my left. The illumination is too brief to help me. It doesn't
matter. Twenty years have made me an expert in navigating
darkness. I'll remain without light until your eyes illuminate
the world for me once more.

❖

Other residents of Caballerizas, 4 were unable to add
useful information about the victim or his presumed killer to
what had already been provided by Raimunda Nuñez. Like
her, none of them had spoken to the two men, though both
seemed pleasant enough. The widow's neighbours shared
her sense that the pair refrained also from speaking to each

other in the course of entering and exiting the building. It was suggested to Manuel Arroyo that possibly the victim went out by himself more often the other occupant did. Or was it the other way around? Retrospectively, some neighbours seemed to have difficulty telling the two men apart. The general attractiveness of the pair, in terms of height, physiques and dress, apparently left an impression similar enough to have made it difficult for casual observers to tell them apart. Individualized details of appearance seemed lacking; distinguishing marks that might have helped identifying one man from the other went unnoticed.

Manuel made a point of returning to Caballerizas, 4 several times to conduct a second interview with residents in a different context; for example, to speak with women without the presence of husbands. This tactic failed to elicit further information. Yet the detective remained convinced that someone in the building must have seen or heard something of significance around the time of the murder or during the three preceding months. His suspicion came to centre on the single occupant of the ground-floor apartment located nearest to the street. The middle-aged man initially admitted to being woken by a noise late on the night before the crime. Then he said he was positive the disturbance occurred at least several nights earlier. Repeated questioning failed to make the man in Bajo-E more forthcoming. Though unable to come up with any reason why this potential witness would withhold information, Manuel continued to believe he was not being told the full truth.

❖

Walking toward where I'm to wait for you to finish with tonight's boy, I feel he and not you is the one of significance being left behind. A disconcerting sensation wanes as I move farther away. Only you have the power to possess me across time and distance, I reassure myself. The strange quality of my journey with tonight's boy has no lasting significance, and is unworthy of examination. Already I've forgotten his name again.

I become encouraged at noticing that the streets have dried from the heavy watering that usually leaves puddles to linger long afterward. Plazas that as a rule remained filled with activity every night until nearly dawn have emptied. I smile. Though it would seem reasonable to assume that only a few minutes have passed since I delivered the boy to you, time loses meaning not just for me but for the world in your absence. A day possesses the same value as a year. A week is indistinguishable from a decade. The globe might have spun a million times since I left you.

Cobblestones supposedly cleaned recently have become freshly littered as well as dry. They're sprinkled with a substance that resembles white confetti. Bending to identify one of the scraps by touch, I feel bare brick where the dot shines. I look up. The source of the shredded white at my feet lies in the stars overhead. Their brightness seems undiluted by the city's lights in a way that the clarity of sky doesn't explain. Perhaps I've forgotten the strength with which stars can shine. Perhaps I haven't searched for illumination in the night for several decades. Above Rome and San Francisco and Buenos Aires stars as bright as these have adorned the darkness above me. The points of light over my head begin to swirl in response to the possibility. They might be floating unmoored in a liquid element, they might be drifting in search of new formations. I look down and see that the lights at my feet are swimming in synchronization to those above. With the sensation of walking on the surface of a deep body of dark water, in fear that only faith prevents me from sinking, I follow a trail of illusionary stars.

PART TWO

The hotel where I am to wait for you is an undistinguished establishment in an unremarkable part of the city. We arranged for the room yesterday afternoon, when it became clear your need for another boy would require satisfaction that night. Because the several passports pertaining to me are kept in your possession, you're the one who completes the registry for a room. I remained, by custom, several feet behind you during the process, paying little attention to a matter that isn't my concern, focusing instead on the imminent challenge of securing your next specimen.

I don't recognize the man now behind the hotel desk, who gives the impression of being the owner. He shows no drowsiness despite the late hour. His manner is unusually discreet and pleasant, as though offering the services not of an ordinary hotel but of one renowned for catering with special sensitivity to guests' needs. Handing over my key, he makes a remark that suggests he believes me to be Spanish, though I'm fairly certain none of my passports are issued by this country. In the same tone of polite interest, he asks if I'll be joined by my friend soon.

"Quite soon," I reply, careful to speak in English. As I move toward the stairs, I sense the man behind me reach for the telephone. I climb to the third floor with a suspicion that the hotel is silent not because all its guests are sleeping but because all its rooms are empty. As usual, you reserved one without windows onto the street for me. Break of dawn will be powerless to blaspheme the darkness required to keep my vision pure. Night will return to the world beyond without corrupting my ignorance of passing hours. Your timelessness of your absence will remain untarnished and true.

I suppose you booked the room for an indefinite stay. It's never certain how long it will take you to finish with a boy. Perhaps some of them afford you several more days of delight than others. Perhaps, on occasion, your need is satisfied quickly, regardless of the qualities of the flesh you're given. It's the same to me either way. However many hours might be marked by the crude clock, each experience of waiting for you is similarly endless and equally unbearable. After opening my room, I hang a sign on the door handle outside. In Spanish, English, French, and German, it reads: "Do Not Disturb." The words strike me, in all four languages, as the punch line of a tasteless joke.

Manuel Arroyo's inquiries throughout the neighbour-hood beyond Caballerizas, 4 leave him to believe the two men felt there was slightly less danger in revealing themselves away from the building than inside it. Shopkeepers easily recognize the individual in the victim photo. Nearly all of

them remark that he spoke and understood Spanish better than the man who was usually but not always with him. This companion was never spotted alone. Both men seemed pleasant; neither appeared overtly friendly. Out-of-ordinary behaviour wasn't observed.

A check-out girl at the Supermercado Más noticed that the two men took care to shop for healthy groceries. She connects this detail to their athletic build and attire. In the afternoon, they regularly wore workout clothes: running shoes, full-length track pants, and light warm-up jackets. Apparently, the men didn't relax outside the cafés in the Plaza de la Alfalfa or stop at any of the small bars in the surrounding streets. Their presence had become familiar as that of any foreigners who, for one reason or another, spend a period of time in the neighbourhood. Perhaps they took a few Spanish language courses or attended non-credit art history lectures at the university. The impression they gave of following no regular employment during their stay was unremarkable. People from other places often linger in Sevilla with no other aim than to enjoy its beauty and atmosphere.

Why wouldn't they? *shrug locals with the kind of self-satisfaction in their city that non-Sevilla Spaniards tend to find irritatingly smug. Even Maria del Carmen Vasquez, who might have had a professional reason to know, apparently failed to ask the tenant that she dealt with whether his move to Sevilla was related to work or to pleasure. When Manuel telephoned the real estate agent to check this point, she icily informed him that clients of the calibre attracted to her agency would be apt to take offence at being subject to a vulgar interrogation. She deals primarily with people in possession of private means, investment incomes, and inherited wealth. The distinguished reputation of her agency is largely owing to the discretion it offers. The sharpness of the real estate agent's voice served only to hone what Manuel believed to be a significant question confronting him. Why had the occupants of 2-A spent three months in Sevilla? What was their purpose for being here?*

❖

After noting the presence of the athletic bag deposited on registering at this hotel yesterday, there's no need to see more of the room. I flick off a switch and curl on the floor against one wall. Light would serve no purpose except to expose that you're not here. A bed without you in it is obscene; a pillow unshared by your head, a burning stone. Food contaminates the taste of your last kiss. To turn on the television would be to invite images to taint a votive vision of your shoulders' breadth, the sweep of your back. I will not sleep or eat until undiluted hope and faith have summoned you from absence. I must obey the demands of my vigil. I must honour sentinel obligations. If my prayers for your reappearance aren't pristine, they will not be answered.

❖

One discovery to come out of the initial stage of his investigation baffled Manuel Arroyo in particular. Though examination of the victim's scars determined his mutilation continued in the months leading to his death, he had often wandered freely by himself during this time. He wasn't kept chained within walls too thick to allow screams for help to penetrate. Multiple opportunities to escape his torturer were afforded. What prevented him, on any of the afternoons he strolled alone through the Plaza de la Alfalfa, from reaching out for assistance, from seeking rescue?

As far as Manuel could determine, no one to witness the man on these occasions noted signs that he might be troubled. His behaviour was as unruffled as when he was with his companion. The detective sought the insights of Oliver Ortega on the matter. In situations like the one at hand, the pathologist offered, the victim's failure to seek help is usually the result of his ego having suffered as systematic and sustained injury as his body. Physical and psychological brutalities occur simultaneously, and are interdependent. Each form of damage allows the other to continue.

The victim loses the will to attempt to extricate himself from his torture. He comes to believe he doesn't deserve to be rescued because there's nothing worthy of rescue. Reduced to a non-human state, he is nothing more than material whose sole function is to be enacted upon. For psychological preservation, he forgets any experience prior to the present one. After all, how can a mere thing possess memory? He doesn't allow himself to conceive of alternatives. A different existence would be alien; prospect of one frightening. A condition that by any ordinary definition would be termed unbearable becomes not only familiar but natural.

When Olivier Ortega paused on the other end of the telephone, aspects of his remarks made Manuel aware of several tendencies in the pathologist he hadn't noticed before. The first was that the clinical precision of Ortega's response to a crime, the detached coldness with which the man spoke, seemed to increase in direct proportion to the horror of the deeds. And, after the disturbing nature of such investigations became obvious, the pathologist went out of his way to avoid face-to-face discussion of them with Manuel.

The detective thought specifically of a case several years ago, involving the rape and murder of a three-year-old Triana girl. At the time of that appalling crime and during others almost as unsettling, he had admired what he considered to be Ortega's professionalism and wished his own were as steely. As for the pathologist's preference to confer on such cases by telephone after one or two initial meetings, Manuel had put this down to the man's general social unease. To confer in person during an investigation wasn't strictly necessary. The detective admittedly found it less awkward to use the telephone himself when speaking with someone reluctant to meet his gaze.

But now he wondered at the impulses lying behind behaviour that seemed particularly prompted by incidents such as the Caballerizas murder. Manuel wished he could see the face belonging to the voice which had stated that while the passivity of the victim under consideration might seem extraordinary, it wasn't in the circumstances. In this instance, the detective wished he could look into the eyes of the man upon whose understanding of such psychological phenomena he depended.

❖

I steel myself against the uncertainty that invades me at the beginning of every vigil. It's a test that must be passed. I don't know why I feel especially vulnerable to the forces of doubt tonight. Repeated experience in withstanding such assaults should have strengthened my defences against them. Yet the darkness swarms more thickly than ever before with needling questions about our love. It clamours to know once and for all why I'm no longer enough for you.

Hasn't each of us maintained his physical beauty to the same degree by means of similarly careful diets and equally exacting exercise regimes? Hasn't my devotion to you deepened not despite but rather because of every sign of your passing youth? I count the fine lines at the corners of your eyes and count my million blessings. I cherish a lessened tautness of your skin; my fingers adore the added texture of creases and folds too subtle to be detected by any touch but mine. A sublimely wrought form has been transfigured by time into a far more richly faceted sculpture with the capacity to reward endless appreciation.

Your love for me has failed to evolve in kind; my scarred surface refuses to inspire your ardour. I can remember how your eyes once shone when you beheld me. Erotic contemplation of my sixteen-year-old flesh took your breath away. You were dazzled by the potential presented by my blank torso and excited to investigate possibilities inherent in my unblemished back. Love drew a blueprint in your mind; desire enriched it with detail. I shivered as your fingers traced my skin with preliminary sketches of the vision to be permanently etched by knives. With sensual languor, you prolonged our shared anticipation of the first cut; its prospect stiffened us until we threatened to break.

When you finally took out your instruments and deliberated which one should carve the initial line of your masterpiece, I moaned with the virginal pleasure I was about to receive. The blade's first slice made me come. The slow twisting of a screw into my left calf, penetration by infinitesimally advanced degrees, elicited a series of spasms whose intensity shuddered me from consciousness. I was revived by the splash of your semen at the miraculous appearance of blood more brilliant and viscous than you had dared dream. Carnally crimson, sexually thick.

For several years, your attentions to my body at those intimate moments remained fervent, and they occurred with a frequency that left me in an unbroken state of bliss. It seemed clear you were enthralled by the first hundred scars rendered by your artistry. I believed they formed an outline you would take pleasure in filling in forever.

Yet, at some point, you must have made a serious error of creative judgement. Your imagination or the execution of it faltered. Perhaps a single incorrectly placed mark, or one drawn by a knife when a nail was needed, destroyed the vision that shimmered in your head. I searched my skin to detect which scar had ruined it for you. I suspected the mistake might be so miniscule that no eyes but yours could perceive it. I wondered why you had never shared your vision with me, never invited dreams I might offer to enhance its glory. I knew only that you no longer wielded your instruments with the same pleasure or received the same reward from them, though my ecstasy at each touch remained unabated.

I had to take satisfaction in sensations that lingered in my flesh between increasingly infrequent incidents of adoration. I learned to savour each throb and sting as a testament of having received your love. I mourned time's erasure of every ache. Your attentions became careless and brutal when it became unimportant where and how you marked me. A knife no longer sliced tenderly. A bolt no longer entered affectionately. Presenting undeniable evidence you had failed, my flesh evoked your regret then revulsion. I came to share those responses.

Once I had gazed in awe at my undressed image in the mirror, overwhelmed by its reflection of my lover's skill and talent. I felt certain I was in the process of being made so beautiful you would never leave me. I imagined I was able to glimpse the completed vision my skin would eventually display. Did each scar depict a star? Clusters formed constellations? Patterns of Pisces, arrangements of Aries? Did you dream of one night embracing all the heavens when you held me in your arms?

With time, I grew to feel responsible for the disappointment I had become. Perhaps my failure to respond to your caresses with due gratitude prevented their perfect manifestation. Perhaps at the critical moment, I cringed or twisted away from your knife, causing it to miss its proper mark. Perhaps my flesh lacked the qualities which would allow it to display your art in all its wonder. Perhaps you made a mistake in choosing me. Whatever the reasons for them, I accept and understand the consequences.

My ravaged skin must always be covered in public to prevent the eyes of the world from witnessing a mess of unsightly scars. Your instruments must stab blindly to obliterate traces of botched beauty that mock you. You must be given flesh as unmarked as mine once was; you must have the chance to fulfill your vision anew; you must be afforded the opportunity to avoid mistakes made with me. It has been the least I can do to find fresh material for you again and again. It has been the only way for me to hold on to your love.

Still, on those troubling nights when only your bitter draught releases me into sleep, I've sometimes wished you were inspired to dig your implements deeper beneath my surface than you've ever conceived of going. To delve beyond a thick wall of toughened tissue until reaching the deepest, darkest chamber of my self where the truth about our love hides. The same dark cave from which occasionally emits a faint murmur, in which occurs a subtle stirring triggered apparently by my seeing small children at play in the park, by hearing their high, clear calls across a street. Though the darkness of this room contains no such prompting sights, and though the silence surrounding me is complete, that inner voice fills my ears now. Unlike in the past, it insists on being heard. It refuses to be disregarded.

❖

It was past midnight in the apartment on Menendez Pelayo where Olivier Ortega lived alone. The rooms beyond the light at his desk lay empty and dark. From the street below reached the sound of traffic moving away from the river, voices of men heading toward the Trastamore bars. They passed in short sleeves beneath orange trees spaced six meters apart along the sidewalk. At the end of October, the nights were still warm. Olivier shivered. A phrase he'd used in his most recent discussion with Manuel Arroyo of the Caballerizas case echoed in his mind.

"Unbearable by every ordinary definition," he'd said to emphasize the objective horror of the victim's existence. He wondered whether the phrase implied there was room for another interpretation of that life. Say the victim's own vision.

Perhaps, according to his definition, there was no horror to flee and, therefore, no reason to appear to eyewitnesses to be in need to rescue. In the context of a sadomasochistic relationship, his emotional well-being could have depended on the physical pain he enjoyed. He might have rejected being assigned the label of victim. He may have felt he was the one in control.

He forces his torturer to give him what he wants, needs, demands. His pleasure derives as much from wielding psychological power as from receiving physical pain. Was he the only one of the pair viewed strolling through the Plaza de la Alfalfa by himself because the inflictor of his pleasure had been forbidden to leave their apartment alone? Wandering beneath the orange trees, he savours knowing his slave cowers in confinement with only knives and ropes and nails for company, with just the prospect that his hands will be soon commanded to use them according to exact instruction, whether wanting to or not.

Olivier reached for a pen to make a note of these possibilities in the case file on his desk. He switched off the lamp at his elbow instead, then flexed his fingers in the dark. The voices of men in search of satisfaction below his window seemed louder when listened to without light. Terms and definitions sprinkled through the papers on his desk seemed drained of power by obscurity. The darkness stirred with words freed from the constraints of clinical psychology, liberated from the chains of pathological theory.

"There is the lover and the loved, and they come from different countries." *The quotation escaped from the black cave of Olivier Ortega's mind and swelled in the darkness around him, expanded to occupy the night beyond. A dozen words hovered like a benediction above strangers in search of each other's country amid the orange trees. Does a loved man have no wish to escape an adorer but only desire to prevent his return to an alien land?*

❖

The sound inside me persists until I recognize what makes it. The inner shifting continues until I have to envision its source. I must admit what I already know. A boy has huddled in the darkness beneath my skin for twenty years. His body has never been wounded; his skin remains unmarked. I've willed myself to deny his existence. I've forced myself to ignore his stubborn presence. It would have been unbearable to acknowledge an imprisonment lasting for several decades without light. To heed the inmate's complaining kicks at his long confinement. To answer his murmur at being wakened by children calling in voices as pure and high as his liberated voice would be.

For peace of mind, I've told myself that he occupies a cave too deep to access, beyond reach of my comforting or rescue. Now I feel his purposeful presence just under the surface of my skin and know he's been this near all along. Except when retreating far below to save himself from sharp blades and invading points of steel, he's hovered beneath the thinnest membrane. He longs for my lips to invite him into the air above where he might breathe again. His stifled voice begs for the chance to speak freely once more. He wants to stretch his limbs and feel the sun and taste the spring. He yearns to glimpse the stars.

Soon, I promise him now. Soon you'll see that the stars

shine as brightly as the last time you wished on them. You'll know they are as numerous as ever. For the moment, remain where it's safe. Haven't I done my part to protect you so far? Didn't each offering I procured for the knives and nails mean saving you from harm that might occur no matter how deeply you retreat from their penetration? Wasn't every specimen sacrificed on your behalf?

Perhaps my assurances to the boy beneath my skin come too little and too late. After my long neglect of him, he has difficulty in trusting me. He falls silent with suspicion, waits in wary stillness. Curls in my darkness as I curl in this equally dark room. He knows me too well not to doubt my promises and pacifications. He understands I'll do and say anything to keep him quiet. The undisturbed silence essential for my belief in your return must be gripped as tightly as ropes have bound my body when its involuntary thrashing beneath your tools might complicate a precise rendering of your love.

❖

A composite drawing of the presumed killer's face was made with the assistance of Maria del Carmen Vasquez. Manuel's first choice, the Supermercado cashier who had seemed to have gained a strong impression of the man, proved unwilling to help.

"All my customers look the same," she said now. Other people in the neighbourhood seemed similarly reluctant to comment usefully on the suspect's appearance after their initial interview. The detective was familiar with this syndrome. If a violent crime isn't solved immediately, those

in whose midst it occurs tend to prefer the unpleasantness be forgotten. Reminders are detrimental to the quality of daily life and bad for business.

It was precisely for professional reasons that Carmen seemed eager to cooperate with the creation of a composite drawing. A quick arrest would be beneficial in terms of silencing speculation that swirled around a crime linked to her agency. Carmen appeared affronted that an unsavoury character had deceived her discerning eyes. She took pride in an ability to size up anyone who walked into her office at a glance. Her originally conveyed vagueness about the presumed killer vanished. She might forget a name or a passport number, but not a face.

Carmen expressed disappointment with the multiple efforts of the first sketch artist, as well as those of two subsequently enlisted. She wasn't able to explain why none of the drawings accurately depicted their subject. Each facial feature might match her memory, yet the composite remained unsatisfactory. She implied the fault wasn't hers, although she didn't doubt that all three artists were highly respected in their field. Was the nose narrower or broader, the eyes spaced closer or farther apart? Lips thinner or fuller? Chin more square? Cheekbones less sharp?

"It really doesn't look like him," Carmen repeated with increasing impatience, shaking her head at the artists' various attempts. "He was much more handsome."

The sketch determined to be the best proved of limited value. It failed to trigger fresh memories in witnesses of the suspect. Some of them thought the drawing was of the victim, though they hadn't suffered such confusion before.

This phenomenon occurs from time to time, Manuel

Arroyo realized. Certain faces, including, and perhaps especially, striking ones escape capture by the lens of camera or memory or eye. Each feature, as well as their arrangement in combination, is inherently elusive. It doesn't really look like him, *thought Manuel Arroyo whenever he studied a photograph of the son he'd last seen ten years before. Unlike the suspect's composite, the snapshots of Jose were in colour. This didn't seem to help the images to reveal the vanished boy. In some, his hair appeared light brown. In others, dark blond. His eyes were now grey, then green. His teeth were always very white. Manuel rarely looked at the snapshots anymore. Soon after it was made, the sketch of the Caballerizas suspect would, to a large extent, become similarly disregarded for being an ineffective investigative tool.*

❖

Slowly, deeply, I inhale darkness until it banishes the doubt queued to come at the onset of your absence. Surely my misgivings have been no more serious and no less fleeting than usual. Uncertainty is silenced; suspicion muted as the presence beneath my skin. That subdermal boy is obviously inimical to us. He must seethe with envy of my intimate knowledge of your lips, my unmatched experience with your touch. In the darkness he has plotted how he can poison me in your eyes. In solitude he schemes of supplanting me by seducing you with his unmarked skin. He would flaunt that flesh like a wanton back-alley whore.

I cringe at having allowed myself to be tricked for an instant by his treachery. He's as insignificant as any offering I bring you, including the current one. Then I smile triumphantly into the darkness.

After finishing with a specimen, no unappeased appetite remains to gnaw you. A fresh cycle in another city begins for us. For nearly three months, you're entirely mine. As happy as I am, equally content. Days are mostly enjoyed within our spacious, well-appointed rooms. Stares directed at us in the street make you uncomfortable. Though carefully covered from undeserving eyes, our bodies still make them widen and shrink in wonderment. We don't go to bars or to the movies. Neither do we adorn restaurants nor relax at sidewalk cafés.

Satisfaction in each other requires no external stimulus at this perfect point. Alcohol and nicotine and other drugs are refrained from. Supremely acute senses can't be heightened further; it would be foolish to dull their unassisted capacity for delight. Newspapers and magazines exist as unsought diversions. Television goes unwatched; the Internet is ignored. The only books I read are tourist guides containing clues to where specimens can likely be found when the necessary moment arrives, and the language texts key to securing the prey.

My sole unaccompanied excursions are taken to confirm the value of hunting grounds suggested by my research. None of these preparations interfere with my pleasure in our present life; they might be measures taken in advance of a distant incarnation on an unborn star. That you now reveal no signs of dissatisfaction with our love cements my confidence in its enduring strength. You never comment on or seem to notice the guides and grammars I study. My brief absences to explore a city apparently fail to evoke your attention.

We feed each other. Considerable time and attention is spent preparing meals from ingredients whose precise combination maximizes strength, health, and beauty. Complex carbohydrates, vitamins and minerals, proteins and fibres and fats: these we ingest in calibrated quantity according to an unvarying schedule. The routine is rapturous. Our only consistent joint venture beyond our rooms is to a gym.

We time our workout for when the facility is least busy. For these sessions, we both wear loose-fitting track gear with long sleeves and pant legs that conceal our lean smoothness, the swollen muscles upon which one risen vein pulses a promise. Gazes of other athletes go ignored until our second month in their midst, when responsive flicks of your eyes offer me hints as to the variety of beauty that will soon inflame your appetite. That day seems an abstraction still. Our bodies remain a secret to be shared only with each other.

After returning home and showering, we spend two or three hours summoning sensations from flesh finely tuned to answering each erotic call. For fleeting instants, between a violent slam and a heavy blow and a forceful thrust, your touch conveys an approximation of tenderness.

❖

Among the few uses made of the composite drawing of the Caballerizas suspect, despite its dubious value, was to include it in the case file sent to the appropriate Swiss authorities, as well as to those of a number of other European countries. North American crime units with focus on missing or fugitive nationals were also made aware of the murder in Spain. None of these countries had knowledge of any cases, open or closed, which appeared remotely connected to the crime.

❖

Relief at having redrawn the beautiful design of our life together sends vibrations through my flesh that soothe the boy inside to sleep. I hum steadily in the darkness at recognizing anew that with time you've intensified your efforts to preserve our happiness. The increased brutality of your attentions to my body has been neither senseless nor needless. It is purposeful punishment exacted on my committing errors whose repetition might cost us everything. There's no pleasure for you in twisting in a knife on those corrective occasions. You would prefer not to have to drive a disciplining nail so deep.

It humbles me that you believe I'm worth your taking such measures, and I receive my instruction with gratitude. Once I must pay the price for bringing you a specimen whose undressed body is revealed to be rotting with disease. Once I'm at fault for delivering a boy whose fear of love makes him try to escape from an experience with you; once for a boy who incomprehensibly fights off your sublime advances.

In a moment of unforgivable thoughtlessness, I leave our rooms one afternoon in a t-shirt that leaves my arms exposed. During another reconnaissance expedition, in an act of unacceptable arrogance, I purchase a braided brand of coloured thread I believe you'll enjoy seeing on my wrist. The consequences for my worst wrong-doings are so severe that several weeks of recovery can be required before I'm presentable enough for public display.

One of these corrections came after a handsome man called my name across the street while we were on our way to the gym. I was certain I'd never met him. I was sure I hadn't dishonoured the name you baptized me with by sharing it with a stranger. I'm not always aware of having made a mistake, nor do you always explain how I've failed. If I were more devoted to our love, I'd know why. It sometimes seems that I'm failing to learn from your patient instruction and committing more frequent errors with time. And with time you've grown to understand that the gravest punishment that can be offered me is to be deprived of your touch entirely.

Even a savage stabbing is withheld. During the past several years, whole months have gone by when the instruments have not been taken out. On one of the earliest of these deprivations, desperate to experience what I'd been without for too long, I sliced my flesh with your sharpest blade. Only a feeble feeling accompanied the emergence of pitifully pale blood. Your love alone can wound me wondrously; attempts at self-satisfaction can offer merely ersatz sensation. In this dark hotel room, my body is deadened with disuse, heavy from having gone unhandled for several weeks. I try to recall the error that resulted in the absence of your recent attention. How serious was my mistake? How severe will my punishment prove to be this time?

❖

Twenty photographs of the victim lay scattered across Olivier Ortega's desk. Some depicted fairly large areas of the mutilated body; others showed one or two fresh wounds in tight close-up. For several evenings, the pathologist had being training his attention on the injuries that were healed. Notations indicated an approximate age for each scar and the weapon likely used to inflict the original wound. Olivier believed that in the arrangement of the marks lay a key to the mind of the man who made them.

They hold individual meaning but are more significant for contributing to a larger design. Each forms one word of a confession, a manifesto, a communiqué. Together, they might reveal the whole map of a mental geography. Oliver views the photos of the scars from various distances and points of perspective. He looks at them under brighter or dimmer light. His eyes float in and out of focus. He waits for a revelation, a reward. The scars will speak if paid sufficient attention. They're waiting for ears that long to hear their message, for a mind that will receive it with sympathy. Olivier's mind?

He considers Egyptian hieroglyphics. Chinese characters. Aztec symbols. Graffiti, code, runes. Scent from the orange trees below his window perfumes his study with possibilities. Maybe it was a mistake to consider the victim's skin as a substance that needed to be destroyed. Olivier tried to see farther, to understand more. He strains to glimpse a dark form hovering beyond a veil of leaves. A living canvas beckons to be transformed by art. A blank surface asks to be made beautiful. The infliction of pain is an inevitable yet incidental component of a particular aesthetic process, like needle pricks in the application of a tattoo.

It's important for the artist to keep his work concealed until it's finished. The world's unwitting eyes must wait. Great patience is required; secrecy is paramount. Plan carefully, execute with brazen caution. Feel your canvas breathe. Let your tools become complicit. Not yet. Soon. Almost. Now.

An act of murder occurs upon placing the final touches on a deeply imagined vision. Death occurs at the moment any masterpiece is realized. The artist's material holds no more life for him. He can't give more of himself to it. The fate of his rendered vision, the world's skewed response, lies out of his control and beyond his concern. Done work is dead work. How quickly life drains from it, how swiftly what was warm turns cold. There's intense sadness that a rewarding journey is over. Exhaustion follows the long, difficult labour. Perhaps the artist experiences an extended period of depression before he becomes inspired to embark on a new canvas. When he does pick up his tools again, the wonders created with them in the past have already been forgotten.

As though transmitting a signal across a vast distance, from some time-zone inhabited beyond the reach of memory, the cell phone on Olivier Ortega's desk indicated with a beep that a voice mail or text message was being left for him. Another communication from Manuel Arroyo, no doubt. He had been calling frequently, and more often as his investigation of the Caballerizas case unfolded. Yet Arroyo had few fresh discoveries to share. He almost seemed to believe that Olivier could provide him with insight into evidence still not unearthed. Into motives for a deed that lay beyond interpretation. The recent murder appeared to be troubling the detective not only because it was proving difficult to solve.

Olivier had glimpsed him on Avenida de la Constitución the other day. The tall, large man was shambling along the opposite sidewalk in a suit that Olivier could see was even more rumpled than usual. He watched Manuel blunder into the combs and bangles laid on a cloth by a Moroccan street vendor. As a trolley moved down the middle of the avenue,

Olivier recalled something about the man its passing hid from his view. A scrap of incomplete knowledge, one briefly insistent note, clanged like the train's bell in his mind.

Before Oliver had begun working with him, Manuel had lost a son. How and why and precisely when? The trolley had passed, and the detective had no longer been in view on the other side of the avenue. Olivier glanced back at the photographs of mutilation on his desk. His vision of what they might have to say was also gone. In his mind lingered the echo of an insistent note of incomplete and then lost knowledge. The scent of citrus in the room remained strong. It insinuated to Olivier that what he had partially understood and almost recognized was related not only to the man seen across the street or the photographs spread over his desk.

❖

I transmit signals to you through the darkness. Egg you on to plunder and feast, urge you to drench yourself with juices. Devour completely. Leave no crumbs to litter the perfect line of your lips. My signal trains on the progression of your pleasure with a precision that excludes the material to inspire it. My cross-haired aim spares me contact with sensations that cause him to cry out as he clutches sheets on which I've groaned. Freedom from feeling what he feels is the sharp-shooter's reward: my flesh is saved from envying his. Jealousy would overburden solitude whose weight is oppressive without it.

I ought to be grateful for the indifference gained by my disciplined focus. It's all I'm allowed at the moment; it should be enough. But my greedy hands want more. They snatch scraps of unsanctioned satisfaction. Furtively,

I fondle the fate of the boy who flails beneath your touch now. Caress the preordained truncation of his time spent in an aura I inhabit through the ages. Twenty or forty hours with you will leave him longing for more. Again and again he'll return to the embankment where he was found in hope of being brought back to you.

Soon the river no longer flows to row a boat upon but to wait beside. After twenty or forty starving nights, unable to withstand his hunger longer, he'll retrace the route by which I led him from the bank. He passes through a succession of three plazas known all his life but made unfamiliar by an experience that has transformed the whole world into alien landscape. He enters a labyrinth of twists and turns without realizing that he'll never emerge. In a narrow street, adjacent to a closed and gated church, he bows before a heavy wood door studded with brass.

A dozen monks chant prayers beyond the thick wall behind his back as he wonders which among a collection of buzzers connects to the rooms where your mouth opened his. Memory of your exploring tongue clouds his mind's clear water, reduces it to mud into which gaudy red flowers sink. They're already enveloped by the muck; their rot curdles his senses. He rings each buzzer, but no one answers and no one lets him in. Bells clang from the top of the church beside him and startle a hundred pigeons up into the dark night. The lost boy's eyes aren't raised by the flutter. They won't lift again toward the rippling stars through which you and I have already flown away. Just as only the bird knows the wing, I could tell him, only the wing knows flight.

❖

The games of small boys playing in the Plaza de la Alfalfa stirred waves of air on which pigeons rose and sank. Within a fence of shiny red slats in one corner of the square, younger children played on structures designed for harmless amusement. They shrilled as loudly through the evening as starlings in the trees overhead. The plane leaves filtered the light of lamps, allowed the cafés to shine more brightly. Across from Manuel Arroyo, beside the newspaper kiosk, stood another that sold fresh-cut flowers.

If twenty years were snipped from the stems of time, any of the darting boys nearby might have been his son. They were dressed in the retrospective style of that era, as though their mothers strove to refashion a simpler time from whole cloth. Clean white shirts with short sleeves, short pants of plain blue linen, outfits ironed as smooth as the limbs emerging from them.

Jose Manuel went to work in an Ibiza bar for his eighteenth summer. A season of island excitement before starting university in Sevilla in the fall. Having a great time, *read his single postcard from Ibiza. In a postcard sent from Barcelona in October, Jose said he'd come there with some new friends met during the summer. He didn't mention university. A third card from Madrid at the end of February said things were going well. After that, silence.*

It came as no surprise that the department for missing persons would fail to deem the matter warranted investigation. Adult children have no obligation to keep parents informed of their whereabouts. To wander without staying in contact with home may be a typical, if unfortunate tendency in youth, but not one to merit alarm. On a professional level, Manuel realized that in absence of evidence of his son being in danger, without indications which might raise suspicion or alarm, an official search was unwarranted. Personally, he felt differently. Yet his wife was opposed to him enlisting a former colleague, now in the private sector, to look into the matter.

Isabel was as adamantly—and incomprehensibly, he thought—against Manuel going to Ibiza with the hope of uncovering clues that might lead to Jose. She suggested he had kept the boy on too short a string for too long. It wasn't surprising the leash would break.

"Jose's gone for now," she said. "I'm here for good."

One of the flyers made up for the Caballerizas case, with a photo of the victim's face and details of his description, lay on the flagstones near the detective's feet. After being questioned thoroughly and repeatedly about the man who apparently passed several hundred times through their midst, habituates of the plaza seemed eager to avoid Manuel. No one shared the bench on which he was sitting tonight. He felt himself the sole occupant of a zone created by a palpable aroma of unease clinging to his clothes.

His presence in the Alfalfa this evening wasn't inspired by a sense that anyone here necessarily had more to tell him. The place itself might speak, if he remained receptive. As the shapes of the dunes on Ibiza beaches, the music of clubs reaching toward the water, might have given up hints of Jose. He might see how a man nearly his son's age lifts his eyes in search of starlings shrieking in the planes. How the sound induces his hand to touch the shirt beneath which tortured skin is concealed. Does he wince? Does he smile? A ball rolled to rest at the detective's feet. A woman reached down and tossed it to a small boy. She removed her eyes from his dash in the direction of the flower kiosk just long enough to gesture to the flyer on the flagstones.

"He sat here and watched the children," she said, without looking at Manuel. "I didn't see him often, but more than once. Enough times to notice his face. He would look at the playing children with the expression of someone confronted by a sight that makes them forget who they are or makes them remember who they were. He would watch from where you're sitting, with your expression. He never stayed for long. Excuse me."

The woman moved off toward the flower kiosk. Was she apologizing for what she had said or for leaving? Manuel reached for the flyer at his feet. Folding the piece of paper this way and that, he fashioned it into an airplane.

"The secret of flight is in the wings," he would explain to Jose. It seemed he hadn't forgotten the secret. His paper plane sailed above the plaza, floated toward the enclosure in which children climbed and swung and leaped. The birds had fallen silent in the plane trees overhead. At eight o'clock, they were sleeping; below, the children continued to play.

The silence of my dark room is broken by a series of sounds from beyond the door. Perhaps a chambermaid is passing up and down the hallway with fresh linen and towels for the rooms to either side of mine. Does she pause outside my door to consider the Do Not Disturb sign hung there? A bucket clangs like a bell to signal the resumption of activity. At first it's comforting to feel I'm not alone in performing a duty. Then I remember my impression on arriving at this hotel that all the other rooms are empty. Maybe the chambermaid is engaged in an unnecessary task. Maybe my vigil is similarly without purpose. No rooms need cleaning; no God requires attention.

The activity of the chambermaid, to a useful end or not, suggests morning has arrived. I resist reaching for a small, hard object in my pocket. I avoid checking the time illuminated on its face. I must save myself from being confronted with the number of hours you've been apart from me. Sounds in the hallway fade; my dark room reverts to silence. As I appreciate anew the blessings offered by this void, another disturbance occurs. The sound comes from inside my room, from inside me.

The chambermaid has woken the boy beneath my skin and drawn him back up to its surface. Alerted to morning, he wants to open his eyes, to stretch, to eat. Go back down where you were, I order him. Go back to sleep. You know it's not safe for you up here. He disobeys my warning. He wails as hopelessly as the prisoner who knows that no one beyond the thick walls of his dark dungeon will hear him. My belly groans loudly to drown out his futile cry, as well as the insistent demand of hunger that he's wakened, that I'm forbidden to meet.

❖

What about the killer's skin? Was it as mutilated as that of the victim? Did one man wish to replicate the design of damage carried by his body in order to create an equally marked twin? Their skin's shared condition might draw them closer together, unify them against an unscathed world.

Manuel Arroyo's interviews suggested that the suspect wore clothes as concealing as those of his victim, and that the two men looked enough alike to have caused some confusion between their identities.

Or perhaps the victim was given marks their creator had dreamed in vain of receiving himself. For years he had hoped and waited for his unscarred skin to become adorned by evidence of a lover's touch. His flesh cried out for a cut's kiss, longed for the bliss of a blade. His body's blank surface taunted and tortured him until he was compelled to enact the role of inflictor that no one would play for him.

Olivier Ortega lifted his eyes from photographs of the victim. He didn't need to look at them anymore. He had memorized the placement and appearance of each wound and every scar until he could feel their mirrored arrangement on his own skin. He rose stiffly from his desk. He hadn't been outside his apartment for several days. His voicemail box was filled with messages not listened to.

Oliver undressed, then stood in front his bathroom's full-length mirror. The unfamiliar sight of his naked body startled him; he tried to ignore it while showering. He searched his skin for scars. Only two were visible; both were faint. One on his left elbow revealed it had been broken by a fall from an apple tree at six. A smaller one showed where his forehead had banged several years later into the sharp edge of a stone wall. His flesh contained no further souvenirs of injury or other damage. It was smooth, taut, toned.

Olivier ran and swam and played tennis regularly in order to sleep soundly and to remain physically fit. Though his manner and dress suggested a man in middle age, the mirror reflected the body of one still young. He was only thirty-five. Already thirty-five. Too young not to burn for

a lover's touch, too old never to have really received one.
Olivier leaned closer to the mirror. His skin appeared flushed
as though from exercise, or with embarrassment, excitement,
or desire. One hand reached toward the reflection then drew
back. To touch the glass might smudge it, mark it.

❖

Don't be frightened, wordlessly whispers the boy beneath my skin, as though I were the one crying to be comforted a moment ago. Nothing's wrong, his murmuring assures me. Is there a note of slyness in the sound? Never mind. He's right. This vigil is no different than any of the sixty which preceded it. I've borne the darkness without you for this long before, and have survived other absences as well.

Soon after our arrival to a fresh site of operations, you usually go away for about ten days. My understanding is that you travel to another city to acquire funds needed to sustain our existence. We never huddle within dim, cramped rooms of poor neighbourhoods. We don't subsist on meals prepared from ingredients chosen for their cheapness.

Expansive, light-filled apartments in marble palaces and sleek suites in towers of glittering glass must be costly, as are haircuts in upscale salons, clothes purchased in exclusive boutiques. I comprehend the importance outward appearances play in the success of our operation. A patina of wealth shields us from intrusive questions; money erases doubts. Yet my calculation of the price of our life together is vague. I'm only given a small amount of local currency at a time. I've never had a credit card or a bank account.

How you earn the large sums we surely need is no

concern of mine. Your ability to replenish our funds so quickly garners my gratitude and increases my admiration of you. I've no worry that during your absences you share yourself with strangers. Over time, you've grown completely dependent on my providing you with whatever you need beyond myself. I trust in my intimate knowledge of the subtlest ebb and flow of that desire. Your absences always occur just after you've enjoyed an offering, when satisfaction gained from one specimen hasn't had time to wane and the ache for another has yet begun to build.

I occupy the days without you by working out at the gym to maintain my beauty for your return. A city is scouted, and a grammar book is studied in anticipation of securing future prey. Soon you'll be back with your metal case filled with cash. Once or twice I've faintly wondered whether replenishing our funds might involve only a brief visit to a bank with access to a trust fund or inheritance. An unnecessarily extended absence may form a part of our operations to which I'm not privy.

Perhaps you stay away longer than required to make me aware how empty my life is without you, and to force me to realize anew that I'll do anything to keep you. Such a stratagem is improbable because it's patently uncalled for. My response to your touch is as eager after one deprived hour as after one week. You must know you don't have to go away to keep me. There's no reason for you to suffer an unessential separation yourself.

Invariably, you look exhausted and spent on your return. Without me breathing beside you, you must find it difficult to sleep. Without my support for balance, you apparently stumble and fall. Faint bruises smudge skin that lay unmarked beneath my lips before you went away. They fade as quickly as my questions about your absence. I have absolute faith in the choices you make in shaping and defining our life. I worship a single God. I believe in His all-knowing wisdom and bow to His infinite power. With open mouth, I kneel before Him and receive His sacred seed.

❖

A preliminary toxicology report arrived from Madrid three weeks after the murder took place. It indicated that no narcotics had been actively present in the victim at time of death. Analysis of the liver did show traces of a chemical substance ingested earlier, probably in small, repeated amounts. While further toxicological study was required to identify this substance, it could be confidently asserted now that it played no significant role in the victim's death. The final report from Madrid could be expected in approximately four more weeks.

❖

In these hours of darkness, God, I must hold on to knowledge of Your abiding kindness. I must remember that I suffer your absence by choice. The first time you admitted to a need for another boy, five years after finding me, you offered to share the experience. Available pleasure in a specimen would be doubled if we partook of it together, you explained. Possibilities of positions would exponentially increase; multiple levels of meaning would unfold.

Performing any act with a boy's body, we exchange signals to remind each other that a variation of it has been enjoyed without him. The present becomes enriched by the past, and familiarity is infused with freshness. Secrecy excludes the specimen; collusion draws us more intimately together. Our eyes lock as we feed him simultaneously, as we serve as each other's witness for the double penetration. Afterward, I can testify he wasn't merely your fantasy. You can provide visual details unavailable from my vantage point. How at the first slice of your knife, his flesh shudders precisely as mine did on receiving the original cut. We re-enact erotic scenarios you and he performed while I was resting, and vice versa. The power of a completed encounter becomes sustained almost indefinitely by means of its replication.

I couldn't accept this generous invitation.

Aware of failing you, I'm unable to bring myself to take part in your attentions to another body. You respond to my shortcoming with understanding. You suggest an alternate way for me to participate. A one-way mirror in a bedroom would allow me to watch unseen from the other side. Wiring the space in which you savour a specimen would enhance my visual pleasure.

He doesn't know that while he obeys your orders, you're gazing beyond an apparent mirror into my eyes. He's unaware the gasps you evoke from him are as audible to my ears as yours. You send me the same signals you would if I were in the bed; they serve the same purpose of triggering our shared memory, of strengthening our connection at the moment. We'll still be able to relive an experience afterward through our common knowledge of it.

Once again, I couldn't agree to your proposal.

To see you with another would be more painful than to be with you inside him. Watching a secretly filmed video of an encounter, as you alternately propose, would bring me equal anguish. I cause you further disappointment when I show no interest in listening to you recount details of experiences that my limitations force you to undertake without me. Still you answer my failing with grace. You don't reproach me. You never accuse me of not deserving your love. Your descriptions of delights unearthed from offerings cease.

Subsequent to the understanding we reach, none of the specimens is mentioned by either of us. No references are made to isolated episodes which serve to cement an enduring union. Out of love for me, you have sacrificed receiving full satisfaction to be found in youthful flesh. From respect, you accept the compromise imposed by my limitations. At the same time, you've made it clear that no further challenges to your wishes are permitted. None.

❖

Once the Trastamore was infamous for its cheap pensions seething with soldiers on three-day passes, and with drunken sailors off the ships of Cadiz and Algeciras. At night they stalked the vicinity, more dimly lit than other areas of the city, twitching for quick release during their short time in a place where opportunities for it might be snatched. Transvestites tapped jittery heels over the cobblestones; boys for rent lurked in the shadows beyond bodegas. The bars were marked only by a single red bulb burning above the entrance. You had to ring a bell and be inspected through a peep-hole in the door before being judged not a threat and admitted inside. There a cliché of queens would shriek with laughter as they ignored the night's tough trade and hoped the next Federales to raid the joint would at least be handsome.

Some of Manuel Arroyo's earliest cases had brought him to the Trastamore of those days when murder seemed mundane as Monday morning. The area had changed considerably in the twenty-five years since. Seedy pensions had given way to smart flower shops, and music from open doors and windows of bars filled the brightly lit streets. Alone, in pairs, or in larger groups, young men sauntered along the sidewalks.

For several evenings, the detective's investigation of the Caballerizas murder had been concentrated here. He visited the cafés and clubs. He questioned doormen and bartenders and waiters. Flyers of the victim were distributed widely. It seemed the man hadn't visited the Trastamore, by himself or with a companion, at least not regularly and probably not at all.

"If he'd been here, I would have noticed and remembered him," was the consistent response to the flyer. A few men mentioned seeing the victim in the streets beyond the Trastamore, both alone and with a man of similar good looks and build.

"Try Itaca," they shrugged. Manuel knew the club, the largest and most notorious one in the district, from investigating several cases in the past. When he visited it now, at one o'clock on Friday night, the place was nearly empty. A dance floor dominated the main area. Porn was projected in giant dimensions on one wall of a separate space to the rear, with steps leading up to a curtained-off dark room at the back.

After speaking to the staff with few results, Manuel returned to Itaca at five o'clock on Sunday morning. This *time, the club was too crowded and too loud to permit any kind of effective questioning. House music pounded. The press of male bodies was unrelenting, the darkness disorienting, smoke asphyxiating. After an unpleasant hour, the detective left a stack of victim flyers near the coat-check and stepped outside. A number of men were scattered beyond the doorway in small groups as well as singly.*

Manuel gulped several lungfuls of fresh air, then lit a cigarette and listened to his ears ring. He realized his unease inside the bar had been much more intense than that experienced in the past. What change in attitude might account for this deeper level of discomfort? Would it lead him to pursue the Caballerizas investigation, here in Itaca and in other Trastamore haunts, less vigorously than he should? What was the shape of the fear that had stopped him, fifteen years ago, from ignoring his wife's wishes and going to Ibiza to see what he could find out about Jose there? House music continued to emerge muffled from the club to his back. The insistent Ibiza sound. The beat that carries across the island's beaches, above grave mounds of dunes. Manuel shook his head in a gesture of denial. An hour in Itaca had left him depressed as well as disturbed.

It was surprising how poorly dressed and groomed most of the clientele of Trastamore bars appeared. How out of shape the men looked. A reaction based on a stereotypical image of the gay man's careful presentation of a painstakingly maintained physique? Glancing down at the rumpled shirt covering his incipient paunch, Manuel grimaced. He flicked his cigarette away and started toward his car. One of the nearby loiterers approached. As though to rebuke the detective's general impression of the Trastamore crowd, this man was noticeably well dressed and well built. He told

Manuel he'd often seen the victim, always with a workout partner, in a gym on Amor de Dios.

❖

I could easily sacrifice the boy beneath my skin to you. Encourage him to emerge from below and assume my place on the surface while I take the one he's occupied in the depths. His flawless flesh would incite you to endlessly prolonged pleasure; the innocence in his eyes would excite your adoration afresh. Instead of retreating beyond reach of knives, I'll position myself to share his experience of their delight. I'll feel your touch as if for the first time. For the first time, I wonder what point there is of keeping the boy below in darkness, of protecting him from love. Wouldn't he thank me for saving him from struggling for several more decades to hold on to faith that soon he'll see stars that dazzle as brightly as your eyes?

❖

Passing from her apartment toward the street door of Caballerizas, 4, Raimunda Nuñez de Guerra Moreno noticed the occupant of Bajo-E looking into the outermost courtyard from his window. His apartment was the smallest in the building, the only one without windows giving onto the street. The two dim rooms were once occupied by a portero; their location near the street door would allow him to monitor movement through it. Doormen had largely become figures from Sevilla's past, however.

Nothing's been the same since '92, *the widow thought once more. Since the murder in 2-A, Caballerizas, 4 certainly wasn't the same. More than a month afterward, the apartment in which the crime occurred remained sealed by the police, though further searches hadn't been conducted inside recently. It was several weeks since the detective in charge of the case had visited the building. He asked Raimunda the same questions and was given the same answers as during previous interviews.*

She didn't know whether Manuel Arroyo also spoke to her neighbours again. The incident in 2-A wasn't discussed by residents of Caballerizas, 4. Interaction between tenants, normally polite but not profuse, was reduced to a passing nod on the stairs or in the courtyards. After noticing the occupant of Bajo-E at his window several more times, Raimunda would have liked to ask whether anyone else saw him there. Some aspect of the man's repeated presence unsettled her.

He seemed neither to hear the sound of her heels approach nor to see her pass. Although she lingered for a moment near the street door, his gaze remained fixed on the fountain at the centre of the courtyard. She had the impression he was intent on watching the fountain until it might begin to flow. Until his attention induced water to play, invoked splashing to fill a void of silence. Raimunda could hardly request that the occupant of Bajo-E stop looking at the fountain in the courtyard. The man was quiet. He appeared properly dressed. The window afforded his rooms their only natural light. His door was kept correctly closed.

❖

Toward the end of one of your ten-day absences or during one of my vigils in a dark hotel room, I sometimes become bothered by a sense that unwanted knowledge is trying to impress itself on me. When your immediate influence wanes slightly, and my mind has become weak without you, a sound repeats inside my head. Although the persisting series of four syllables demands to be understood, I doubt I could make it out if I wanted to.

The sound must derive from one of the languages whose rudiments I learn then forget as my need for them comes and goes. I know the state of non-existence in which I passed my first sixteen years on earth was devoid of language of any kind. Eagerness to please my rescuer made it easy for me to master the English we speak to each other in public as well as the private idiom we share while alone. Our language of love is the one I'm most fluent in, and the one out of which my thoughts and dreams are formed. Its vocabulary is limited to simple expressions of desire and need, duty and command.

If my spoken English sounds slightly different than yours, I've supposed that owes to my having to communicate to a greater degree in the various languages of specimens in order to secure them. As the quartet of syllables begins to chime like an interior bell through the present darkness, imagination makes me wonder whether its inarticulate voice is flavoured by the same accent as mine. The boy beneath my skin cries out like his name is being called; the sound immediately stops, as though all it wanted was to receive a response. I curl more tightly around myself. The heaviness that settles over me reminds me of occasions when I would waken, during our early years together, with a sense that a day possessed special weight, though no celebratory landmark of my life with you had arrived.

❖

At midnight, Olivier Ortega stepped from his apartment building and moved down Menendez Pelayo wearing a white t-shirt, jeans, and sneakers. He doubted he had dressed this way since the age of sixteen. The unfamiliar clothes felt tighter and more revealing than he knew they were. Although this street ran straight, the trees spaced along it seemed like signposts marking the way forward in a journey which would be complicated without them. Leaves overhead nearly hid fruit that in November hung small and green. By January, it would mature into globes gaudily orange as the uniforms of men who were cleaning the pavement with powerful streams of water now.

The Trastamore seemed strangely subdued for a Friday. Few fresh footprints marked the wet cobblestones. Although he'd never ventured into the area at this time of night before, Olivier had received an impression that a steady stream of searchers usually flowed toward it now. He slowed on approaching several bars then quickened to pass them. When he entered Itaca, the doorman looked at him in apparent surprise. Was he inappropriately dressed? A boy with a platinum blonde Mohawk and several facial piercings leafed through a copy of Fotogramas at the coat check.

"Nothing for me?" he asked, glancing up from a pictorial spread of Angelina Jolie and pretending to pout with disappointment. "You're early, cariño, aren't you? Well, the first bird always catches the juiciest worm." Through a closed door to his right, house music pounded to the same beat that was confusing Olivier's mind. Early? Wasn't he late? Hadn't he arrived here fifteen years too late?

From one end of the coat-check counter, the face of the Caballerizas victim looked up at Olivier. Manuel must have

*left the flyers there. The murdered man's eyes had been open
at the moment of his death, as though he wanted to witness it.
They seemed to regard Olivier knowingly—but in invitation
or in warning? He was aware the coat-check boy and the
bouncer were both looking at him with curiosity.*

*"Yes or no?" the former demanded with camp flatness.
"In or out? Which will it be? Make up your mind, cariño."
As he retreated blindly back out into the street, Olivier heard
the boy call mockingly after him. "Don't leave me this way.
Stay with me forever. You know I'd die for you, darling."*

❖

Sounds of activity recur beyond the door. Is a
chambermaid moving up and down the hall again? Has
another night passed, another morning arrived? I haven't
moved from where I curl in the darkness except to feel my
way to the bathroom twice. Water hasn't touched my lips,
food hasn't descended down my throat. I've ignored the
continued whispers and cries of the boy who remains just
beneath my skin. Disregarded his subversive encouragement
for me to give in to temptation by turning on a light, stretching
stiff limbs, splashing cool water on my face.

Once I start doing what he wants, there will be no end
to it. I know he'll ask me to do more and more until I find
myself rowing on rivers and wishing on stars. To my relief,
he falls silent now; most likely in order to listen to the sound
out in the hall. There's something besides the chambermaid
to hear. Two men are involved in a discussion or a debate
just outside the door.

One of the speakers expresses himself mildly; the other
seems more vehement. I can't tell whether either voice

belongs to the owner of the hotel. At the point where it sounds like a dialogue is threatening to turn into an argument, the voices break off in a way that makes me think the subject hasn't been resolved. Footsteps fade. Silence resumes. The chambermaid has apparently finished her work in this part of the hotel, and the boy remains mute beneath my skin. I sense his silence is tactical. Deprived of his voice, I'll realize I've come to depend on it in the darkness. Naively, he thinks I require his company. Mistakenly, he believes he's the one I can't survive without. Not you.

❖

The owner of Gimnasio Sevilla looked exactly like the character of the crusty old manager of the down-at-heels facility where the down-and-out fighter trains for his triumphant comeback in every boxing movie Manuel Arroyo had seen. The man was short and squat and still powerfully built despite his age. Whether his gruff exterior concealed the requisite heart of gold, however, would remain unclear to the detective.

The gym owner brusquely confirmed that the subject of the victim photo had lifted weights there almost daily for the three months leading up to the end of October. Both this customer and the workout partner who was nearly always with him paid a drop-in fee of seven euros on each visit, though it had been pointed out that given the frequency of their attendance, a short-term membership would have been much less expensive.

As a policy, drop-in customers of Gimnasio Sevilla are never asked for personal information or given receipts. The two men had usually worked out for several hours in the early afternoon, when the place tended to be least busy. They clearly knew their way around the equipment; their training regimen was obviously advanced.

"They didn't stand around gossiping like girls the way some of these clowns do," the gym owner growled. All except three of the members in the place on Manuel Arroyo's initial visit were quick to recall the victim and his workout partner, but they had little to add to previous witnesses' impressions of the pair. The two men stayed to themselves and barely spoke to each other. This lack of sociability could have been because they were the sole foreigners in a gym that catered to the immediate neighbourhood. They also approached their workouts seriously.

They always wore full-length track clothes, although shorts with sleeveless or t-shirts were the predominant attire of the place, especially in the hotter months during which they had attended. Because they entered and left the gym dressed for working out, the pair hadn't needed to change in the locker room beforehand, nor did they shower there afterward. If not friendly, they were courteous. They returned weights to the racks after use. They wiped sweat from benches after finishing with them. They didn't linger on equipment others wanted.

The dearth of information regarding the two men offered by the Gimnasio Sevilla disappointed Manuel more than his scantier findings in the Trastamore. From what he had learned of the pattern of their daily life in Sevilla, it seemed clear they were seen in the gym more often, at closer range, and for longer periods of time than anywhere else. The detective was especially frustrated that not a single telling detail of the suspect's appearance or manner had been noted, as far as the members he spoke with would admit.

He felt that more attention had been paid to the two men, and a greater disturbance been created by their presence than was being let on. He sensed a concealed animosity. Did it arise from the intrusion of foreigners upon a space which beleaguered locals felt belonged to them? Tourists whose presence was economically vital to the city could be resented by Sevillanos because of that dependence. Many natives steered clear of Santa Cruz to avoid the throngs of Germans overrunning the barrio; some bars pointedly announced on signs that English wasn't spoken inside them.

Perhaps the attitude sensed by Manuel toward the victim and suspect in Gimnasio Sevilla was partly related to this feeling. But he suspected something more might be at play here. What? The way the two men had kept themselves apart? Their exclusivity?

Weights clanked and banged out another bar of jarring, metallic music. Manuel winced. Heavily mirrored walls confronted him with his reflection everywhere he glanced. Unfamiliar angles and unknown points of perspective offered multiple glimpses of what appeared to be a stranger.

Who was this man in a rumpled suit and scuffed black shoes? Manuel sucked in his stomach and squared his shoulders. What wasn't he seeing here in spite of all the mirrors? He would have liked to ask Olivier Ortega. The usual difficulty in reaching the pathologist had increased of late. In a single voicemail reply to a dozen or so messages from Manuel, Ortega stated he was examining all materials relevant to the Caballerizas murder in his possession and expected to send a complete report on them soon.

The withdrawal of Ortega's attention from the case was palpable and surprising. Intuition that his colleague was especially disturbed by the crime had led Manuel to believe he would be compelled to ponder it with greater rather than less diligence. The detective felt some of his own focus dissipating in the absence of Ortega's full involvement. A difficult investigation had become more difficult. For the first time since viewing the crime scene, Manuel wasn't certain he would solve the question of who was responsible for it, what motives had inspired it, or why it occurred. As though doubt were a virus that runs rampant as soon as it's acknowledged, he wondered for the first time in fifteen years whether he would ever know what had happened to his son.

Suddenly, seemingly from out of nowhere, the sense of having been forced to endure too much darkness overwhelms me. Yet my current experience of being without light doesn't feel like it has lasted longer than previous ones. It's the cumulative weight of all those past occasions spent in obscurity as well as the oppressive anticipation of a similar number still to be burdened that becomes intolerable all at once. If I were brave or foolish enough to murder my desire for the light radiated by your eyes, I would shatter the glass that must be present in the bathroom of this hotel room. With the sharpest shard, I would pierce my unappreciated flesh so deeply that in mercy it would kill the boy inside, no matter how far down he tried to retreat; so profoundly that this act of penetration would register on my senses despite not being executed by your hand. While you continue to savour an expanse of smooth skin across the city, for hour after oblivious hour, my final wound sings in the solitary darkness. Holy hymns provide me solace. I lick blood induced from my depths, draw succour to sustain myself until I'm rewarded by the knowledge that in the end, at the last moment, I'm free of needing you. Capable of returning for good to the original darkness from which you summoned me to life.

No. Not yet. Never.

In the still-overwhelming darkness, my insensate skin taunts my lack of courage to do what's necessary to liberate myself once and for all from longing for light. I attempt to silence the jeers by removing a small, hard object from my pocket again, by focusing on how the only implement realistically available to provide sustenance at this moment fills my hand.

The cell will ring to signal you've finished with the current specimen. It will announce my exile from your eyes is at an end. Within an hour you'll be with me again. There will be just enough time for me to banish doubt from my eyes before you knock on the door. Just enough time to re-adopt the expression of unalloyed acceptance you'll seek on my face. There will have been just enough time for you to perform me the courtesy of scouring the scent of a stranger from your skin. Of eliminating aromas of ardour elicited not by me, but by him. Those of semen and blood, among others.

PART THREE

A powerful blow struck within my belly knocks the air out of it, leaves me fighting for breath. During these recent hours of darkness, I've come to know the presence inside me well enough to realize this kick wasn't one of complaint. A warning? As soon as the question presents itself, I sense the scent of immediate danger in the room. It's not smoke from fire. The threatening aroma emits from me. Something clean and cold and dark mixed with something rich and warm. A distillation, an essence.

My memory is wafted awake. Can this be an olfactory souvenir of the latest offering? Unlikely. His sleeve just brushed mine as I led him to you; his hand rested for a moment on my shoulder once. This contact was insufficient to permit the specimen's scent to permeate my clothes and skin. I feel my way to the bathroom and undress. Fumble in the dark with taps, stand under a scalding shower, scrub myself harshly. The boy beneath my skin must be cringing from the rough treatment and extreme heat inflicted upon it. Perhaps he'll retreat from discomfort, descend back into the depths from which his intrusive voice can't reach.

For me, my flesh's prickling provides slight pleasure, akin to that given by your needles. I step from the shower through steam that feels dense as black water; the room beyond seems pooled with deeper darkness. Waves of unbanished scent still rise from my bare skin. Although I realize the aroma must be objectively pleasant, it sickens me for being the same one in which you currently luxuriate. My stomach heaves as I curl against the wall. Someone is sobbing in the dark. It isn't the voice of the boy beneath my skin, and it can't be me. I haven't uttered a sound of sorrow in fifteen years. I haven't cried in pain since the night, five years after you found me, when I was first instructed to find you flesh. No matter how sharp the instruments used on me, despite the depth to which lengths of pointed steel are inserted, notwithstanding the barbed hooks and the double-blades, I haven't once wept since the night I learned the truth about love.

❖

Late one night, Manuel received a call at home from Olivier Ortega. The psychiatric pathologist stated he would no longer be working on the Caballerizas case. After careful study and thorough response to the materials provided him to date, he felt he could be of no further assistance. Several other matters required his attention. He was scheduled to present a lecture in Salamanca and from there would continue on to Paris to take part in a conference of European Union colleagues.

These commitments had been made well before the murder in Caballerizas occurred; the homicide division knew at the onset that Olivier's involvement in the investigation would be of limited duration, and had surely informed Manuel of that circumstance at the time. Olivier would send in his full report on the case at hand before departing for Salamanca. If the detective felt in need of further assistance from a criminal psychiatrist, he could, of course, seek the services of one of several others who were available to his division. Most likely, such an arrangement had already been made.

Manuel held the phone to his ear for a full minute after it fell silent, as though something remained to be heard. As much as what he said, the tone of Ortega's voice left the detective perplexed. He didn't doubt the pathologist had sound reasons for ending his involvement with the Caballerizas crime. The man's association with the homicide division was flexible in nature. Everyone had too much work and not enough time. Manuel was beginning to receive pressure to move on to more recent cases. Still, Ortega's tone suggested that he might have requested to be removed from the murder investigation at hand whether forced by other obligations or not. Did his customary curtness contain an unfamiliar note of nervousness?

Manuel was used to a certain amount of stiffness in the pathologist's manner and voice. Privately, the detective felt the man needed to get out more. Ortega should get himself laid instead of brooding over case files late at night. This tendency to hang on to cases, including ones officially closed, made Manuel wonder why the pathologist would disassociate himself from an investigation that remained ongoing.

His profession had brought him into contact with crimes

far more disturbing in the past. Was there a particular aspect of this murder that was personally upsetting to Ortega? And to himself? Manuel looked at the phone he was still holding. He thought of calling his wife in Córdoba. Isabel had left him a year after Jose disappeared. Almost to the day. She was long remarried. It was after midnight. A call at this hour would mean an accident, an emergency. She'd be annoyed to be disturbed when all he had to say was that he was fine.

"I'm fine," Manuel said aloud. His words hung in the air around him, then travelled to other rooms of the apartment, searching for someone to receive them.

Though the air remains warmed by steam, and my contaminated flesh continues to burn, I shiver violently. As always, pleasure not offered by your hands turns quickly into discomfort. For the first time since entering this hotel room, I consider the athletic bag deposited here on the afternoon before the current offering was brought to you. It represents the only luggage I'll bring to our next site of operations.

My possessions are few. I don't need much; I need only to keep you. The athletic bag contains little more than a change of clothing. They'll be untainted by the latest specimen's scent, perfumed instead by the soap in which our clothes are washed together. Usually the shirt I wear might be either yours or mine. We're nearly the same size; what fits you fits me. Digging through the layer of clothes at the top of the bag, I encounter several objects unrecognizable to my touch below. You placed them there.

Without turning on a light, I know they're the souvenirs

you always keep of an experience with the most recent specimen. For three months, they've been locked in the metal case to which you possess the only key. Perhaps during my scouting excursions you caress a student ID, a baseball cap, or one running shoe. The scent of fresh ejaculate greets my return one hour later.

The mementoes have drained of aphrodisiac value by the time you're given the next offering. Then new artifacts with undimmed erotic power throb in the metal case. Though holding on to evidence of our operations poses risk, you're unable to let go of stale souvenirs until fresh ones have been secured. Even then, you can't bring yourself to dispose of the useless items. They're placed in my athletic bag for me to toss into a Dumpster near the hotel where my vigil will be performed. This task is to be carried out immediately on my arrival in order to avoid disrupting my prayers for your return.

It's puzzling I could have forgotten to perform the simple duty this time. Small obligations bear the same weight as large ones. My puzzlement transfers from a failure of dispose of the objects to the objects themselves. Usually I try as much as possible to avoid touching and looking at the items while tossing them away, as though they were smeared with excrement. Now I wonder, as distantly as perhaps I once mused on the baffling disappearances of stars, why each boy leaves several articles of probable value to him behind after you've finished with his body.

However dazzled by your touch, though left barely able to see or think from the overwhelming experience, it seems unaccountable that he would stumble away without one shoe, a favourite t-shirt, his wallet. Points of light stir in my mind; swirl into constellations of possibility, demand me to seek further illumination. A state of starvation that might have been indefinitely withstood is made unbearable by the first bite of food. Appetite isn't soothed into submission; it's awakened to fiercer hunger.

I flick a switch. I blink beneath an electric glare that penetrates my skin and causes the boy beneath to shield his eyes. Blinding light exposes the unpardonable nature of my sin against darkness as I remove three items from the athletic bag. A membership card for a rowing club whose photo shows the face of the latest boy I've brought to you. A round gold medallion on a fine gold chain. A wrist band braided from blue and scarlet threads. I close my eyes and stars scatter beneath their lids.

❖

Although Esperanza was twelve, like me, she didn't go to school. She spent every day on her chair at the end of the block, next to the coal man's stall, in front of six steps leading down to the one dim room in which she lived with her sister. Because their cellar didn't have electricity and Esperanza didn't like to work in the gloom, she sat out on the sidewalk with the tray that held her spools balanced across her knees.

The lengths of string were always arranged in the same way by her sister, according to colour, but Esperanza could have found the one she wanted wherever it was on the tray. She could tell colours apart by touch.

"Yellow feels different than green," she explained. Blue was our favourite colour. The skirt and blouse worn each day by Esperanza, as well as the sweater around her shoulders when it was chilly, were all bright blue. Some of her *pulseras* were braided from contrasting shades of blue and some combined blue with other colours. All across the city, I saw boys with blue wrist bands which had been bought in a stall in the Plaza del Duque from a man who paid Esperanza two pesetas for each of them.

Esperanza had to braid a hundred bands a day. Even without looking, with her face turned to the sky, that wasn't hard for her. Her fingers were strong and thin and deft; they twisted and pulled precisely. Her flying hand swooped down to pluck another string from the tray like a bird attracted to some bright, shiny object on the ground. Esperanza's pace didn't slow when I crouched on the cracked sidewalk next to her after school was over, before rowing practise on the river began.

She didn't have to tell me she had been waiting all afternoon for me. Her keen ears let her know when I approached down the block with a piece of meat my mother wrapped in paper for those two poor girls. Esperanza would be already smiling before I drew near.

"I've done forty-six more since noon," she laughed. "I'm almost there." Esperanza believed that when she braided one million bands, she would be free. She didn't say where she was going to go or what she planned to do after her liberation from the sidewalk chair. I imagined her vanishing into a wide, blue sky, in her similarly coloured skirt and blouse, fingers fluttering like feathers. She would soar up toward the sun, which she insisted was blue no matter what I said.

"I can feel it's just as blue as the stars," she repeated

as we both sneezed from dust that drifted from next door whenever the coal man dug into his supply to sell half a kilo to a housewife. The coal smelled dark and heavy and cold. When Esperanza woke each morning, she was covered with a sifting of black, as though in sleep she burned with dreams whose ashes settled over her like souvenirs of what blind eyes can see while closed.

❖

In the days following his late-night call from Olivier Ortega, Manuel moved mechanically through the few steps that seemingly remained to be taken in the Caballerizas investigation. Each one led to a wall as thick as those of the building in which the murder had taken place. The only discovery made by the detective during this time was that of the words he had wished to say to his wife on the night of Ortega's call. We'll never know, *he wanted to admit to her—finally, at last. As the unspoken words repeated in his mind, they sounded less like an admission of the truth concerning his son's fate and more like the confession to a crime.*

❖

Sometimes Esperanza hoped that if she braided extra bands for the day, her sister would feel less sad.

"Maybe one hundred and thirty will make Selena happy," she said, her fingers dancing faster than ever. No matter how hard Esperanza worked, her sister was never able to smile when she returned from the train station each evening. The place was permanently filthy; Selena's mop and broom could never get it clean; a million days of trying wouldn't set her free. Selena moved silently and heavily around the cellar, as though still dragging a big bucket of sour grey water. By candlelight, she inspected the day's newly braided bands for flaws.

Each one had to be perfect to be worth a pair of pesetas. There was no room for mistakes; not an inch of coloured string could be wasted. Esperanza was always careful, and her older sister was always satisfied. Once I asked Esperanza if I could pay her two pesetas to braid a blue band especially for me. I didn't want to buy one made for a stranger from the stall in Plaza del Duque.

"You need to save your money," she laughed in refusal. "Or you'll never make it to America." Although she knew how badly I wanted one, she couldn't give me one for free. Sometimes when her face was turned to me with a dreamy look, I suspected Esperanza was imagining the beautiful blues she would like to braid for my wrist. Her longing to give me the most dazzling band in the world would dye its strings with shades of our favourite colour never seen before. I'd be adorned with the blue of the sun, the blue of stars, with all the brilliant blues the world is too blind to see.

❖

A moment after tying the braided band around my right wrist, I move it onto the left. When the gold chain is fastened around my neck, the medallion rests just beneath my throat. The runners, jeans, and hooded sweatshirt I remove from the athletic bag belong to neither you nor me. Both shoes and clothes prove to be too large, as though they were packed for someone else.

The blue of the sweatshirt is unsettlingly bright. Stowing the rowing club card in the back pocket of the jeans, I wonder whether I might have been especially fond of blue, when I was allowed to have a favourite colour, a preferred season. My eyes insist on closing again. After hours of darkness, the light in the room is too strong and the shirt's blue is too bright to bear.

Raimunda Nuñez Moreno de Guerra continued to watch for the man living in Bajo-E at his window. It's possible to remain alert to one's surroundings without compromising one's sense of discretion, the widow decided. If she had paid more attention to the former occupants of 2-A, she might have been able to be of greater assistance to the detective in charge of investigating the unfortunate incident next door. Awareness that their movements were being monitored by a nearby neighbour could have in some way acted as a deterrent to the crime.

Without making an obvious point of looking toward the apartment nearest the street door, Raimunda kept an eye out for the sight of someone standing at its window. She lingered by her mailbox, directly across the courtyard, to note the name neatly printed on the card attached to the buzón for Bajo-E: Joaquin Polo Bueso. Taking time to chat with the cleaner who started each morning with the outermost patio before moving her bucket and mop to other areas of the building, she learned that the girl shared Raimunda's sense that Bajo-E didn't leave his apartment to go to work.

"He's very quiet," said the cleaner, with a shrug. It struck Raimunda that now the wooden shutters on the window of Bajo-E were always closed. She wondered whether this was because the occupant had noticed her glances. It would be as dark inside his rooms during daytime as at night. From the patio, it wasn't possible to tell whether a light was on in the apartment or not. No sound emerged from behind the closed shutters and door. Yet Raimunda felt increasingly certain someone was in there. Waiting, listening, holding his breath. As she paused beside the fountain in the centre of the courtyard, she realized she was doing the same thing.

❖

My eyes are jerked open. For the first time, the voice inside me is speaking a language, not just making sounds that require interpretation. The syllables seem slurred beyond understanding, as though articulated by lips and tongue left clumsy by long disuse. This speech slowly becomes more distinct until I'm able to comprehend some of its elements. *Cadena. Pulsera. Rojo. Azul. Remo. Rio.* The words sound like prayers of gratitude for a return of light. I recognize the accent of the incantation. Candles glow in the cathedral of my mind, warm stone-cold memory to life, reveal La Macarena.

❖

The Calle Pozo forms a single curved block in a maze of similar suggestions of streets. I stand on a balcony overlooking dimly lit cobblestones two floors below. Beyond the French windows behind me lies the room where I sleep. Red and blue rowing ribbons splash bright colour on white walls. The voices travelling from farther to my rear belong to my mother and father. They're talking in the kitchen.

It must be ten o'clock because my mother is sautéing bread in olive oil and garlic for my father. He asks if there's any ham tonight; she replies with a sigh of indulgence or impatience. The sound of a guitar being strummed rises from below. The crippled man who repairs guitars in a shop on the ground floor of the building is testing the instrument he's worked on today. Again and again, just before I can decide whether it is plaintive or playful, a tune breaks off in mid-phrase.

The balcony across the narrow street seems near enough to touch. An old woman living in the opposite *piso* keeps pots of geraniums there. The flowers' scent is cold and dark and clean. At night it sometimes wafts so strongly across the street, I might be holding the blossoms to my face. The rich warmth of oil and garlic drifting toward me from behind combines with the scent of flowers in front to form a chord that twangs each of my strummed senses.

❖

Now the boy beneath my skin speaks more insistently, more loudly. *Madre. Padre. Casa.* Now the cold, clean scent twining through my mind nudges like my hand urged the latest specimen toward you through a doorway. Whose mother, whose father, whose house? Weren't my sixteen years before you found me spent in a state of non-existence devoid of sight and sound and touch; free of experiences to be remembered, without sensations to be recalled? As a non-being, didn't I lack a name, a language, a history?

I struggle to envision the moment of your original appearance out of darkness in hopes of glimpsing clues to what might have preceded it. I picture you emerging from the mouth of a black tunnel into the lessened obscurity of night. The tunnel is formed by a bridge running above. The bridge connects one side of a river to the other. Perhaps a second bridge lies behind my back, as one runs in front, to contain this time and place as a frame contains a picture. Across the water, above an uneven line of rooftops, the illuminated dome of a cathedral surely rises into the stars. Reflections of coloured lights must be cast on the water from cafés and bars along the banks. Voices must carry over the rippled surface with a clarity that makes me believe I can reach across and touch the opposite side from where they travel.

As you move near toward where I wait, carrying voices and coloured lights become faint. Your eyes seek mine, and a distant dome no longer seeks the stars. When your hand touches my arm, the brilliant light of this original touch turns the world beyond black as a tunnel's depths. Memory of that touch now blots out my flicker of vision of the landscape on which it occurred.

❖

A second and final toxicology report from the national crime laboratory in Madrid failed to identify the traces of chemical substance found in the victim but confirmed a prior belief that it played no direct role in his death. This report cleared the way for the cause of death that had been tentatively established by the Sevilla coroner to be placed on an official basis: a fatal pulmonary episode sustained in the course of violence. Examination of the victim's heart found that the organ had been healthy and strong.

❖

No documents are available to shed light on the identity of the boy I've envisioned being found beside a river. The passport that enables me to travel with you from one site of operations to the next is kept locked in your metal case except during our journeys. In fact, you have several passports for me, each issued by a different country.

I'm certain none pertains to the nebulous identity I held before you found me, nor do I remember signing or being photographed for any passport after that date. My few glimpses of these documents at airport check-in counters and immigration controls and hotel registration desks have led me to believe that each one contains slightly different information. The data to define me is variable.

For the inauthentic world, my name and age and place of birth are subject to change, dependent on your wish or need of the moment. The only truth about who I am has been the one created by you. The name you baptized me with belongs to me in the same way I belong to you. Your arms were my place of birth; my age when you discovered me was the age you needed me to be then.

On rare occasions when a voice that isn't yours addresses me, it might be pronouncing a name as distinct from the same one uttered by your lips as any of the names contained in my various passports. Perhaps the signature in each of those documents is as different as the name it spells; perhaps none of the photographs show exactly the same face and none show exactly mine. My views of passports spread open for official eyes have been too brief and infrequent for me to be sure. You position yourself in such a way that my sight of them is blocked. Whether genuine or not, none of my passports has presented difficulty at immigration points yet. Each seems to satisfy inspection with ease. For my part, I've always been confident of holding certain knowledge of my single, true identity: I am your lover.

The Sevilla Homicide Division received a call from the University of Salamanca in regard to Olivier Ortega. The pathologist had failed to appear for the lecture he was scheduled to deliver there. Nor had he checked into the hotel room reserved for him by the university. A check of the passenger manifestoes of Iberia Airlines indicated that Olivier Ortega didn't travel to Salamanca on either the flight on which he was booked or a later one.

Inquiries made to several other Sevilla institutions to which he was affiliated, including the local university, revealed they hadn't been informed that he had changed his itinerary or cancelled his trip. Three days later, the organizers of the Paris conference of criminal pathologists called to query whether their Sevilla participant had been prevented by illness or other reasons from honouring his commitment to them.

When no word was received in Sevilla from Olivier

Ortega after four more days, a pair of policemen was sent to his apartment on Menendez Pelayo. Neighbours hadn't seen the man recently. His tidy apartment contained no indications to contradict a departure on a short journey one week ago. Manuel Arroyo followed these developments closely. On learning of Ortega's apparent disappearance, he immediately thought it must be connected to the Caballerizas murder. Not in the actual criminal sense, but in a way that was indirect, associative. In the detective's mind, two patently distinct matters became linked as closely as the related aspects of a single case.

"I chose red and blue because they're the colours of the rowing ribbons on your bedroom wall," Esperanza explained. "Whenever you look at this *pulsera*, you'll know you can win. Even in America, you'll be able to come in first or second place." Because Esperanza had braided my band from her most expensive string, its colours would never fade even if worn while swimming in the Pacific Ocean when I reached California. I didn't ask Esperanza how she was able to afford to make me this perfect gift.

"Let me tie it for you," she said, fastening the band around my left wrist. Her touch felt cool. Her fingers lingered for a moment on the vein of my wrist after tying the knot there, as though she was feeling for my pulse, listening to the beat of blood with her keen ears. The sound seemed to make her happy. Esperanza's smile suggested the sun had turned a more beautiful blue. "Run now," she said. "Or you'll be late for your rowing club." As I walked away, she called: "Promise me you'll never take it off. Promise you'll row your boat until you drift among the blue stars."

❖

I finger the braided band around my left wrist, learning how the *pulsera* feels smooth and rough at once. The texture teases me with a promise of having something to teach me. Each woven thread of red or blue holds the strand of an answer. Together they inform me that a need to quench your thirst with flesh that isn't mine didn't gradually grow during the course of our first five years together. The desire was there from the very start, and it was never simply desire for flesh more youthful and less marked than mine.

Your pleasure in specimens has always derived from making me complicit in the act of betrayal; manoeuvring me into being the one who sets each of them up excites you. It all at once seems clear that you'd never have the slightest difficulty in securing sumptuous flesh to feed on. Initial experiences with other boys, probably pleasant, were described as unhappy to delude me into believing my assistance would be required in order to avoid future disappointment. Your hunting skills are exquisitely refined. After all, they enabled you to capture the original, ideal prey in me.

I rub the gold medallion resting coolly below my throat and understand you waited five years to present your system of satisfaction to be certain that by then I would be powerless to resist compliance. Every one of your honeymoon kisses was orchestrated to melt my memory of an existence preceding them. Each unrelenting entry into my body was for the purpose of driving out belief that anyone but you could fill it. All aspects of our life together have been ordered to render my dependence on your touch complete.

I remove the rowing club card from my pocket and study its photo. The face looks serious yet untroubled. Nothing in his features or in his expression suggests why this boy might have disturbed me more than others I've brought you. It's been my belief that all of them are no more than pawns. Easily disposable pieces whose sole value lies in their allowing us to win the tricky game that is our union.

I've dismissed each specimen for his ultimate unimportance. I've despised all of them for their ignorance of this insignificance. Now I know my ignorance has been greater than that of the offerings; it's made me more of a pawn than any of them. I'm almost certain, suddenly, that any pleasure you take in their smooth flesh is desultory at best. You enjoy offerings for the delight of witnessing my pain in procuring them. They serve primarily as an aphrodisiac to heighten your excitement in wielding power over me. You were able to offer to share specimens with me secure in the certainty that I wouldn't accept the invitation. Filming encounters, I see in retrospect, would have meant violating your stringent policy against allowing records of our operations to exist.

You felt safe knowing there was no danger of my wishing to witness your mechanical, almost bored ministrations to each beautiful boy. That is, if you use their bodies at all. After I bring you a specimen, quite likely you do no more than pay him a sum of money too large to be refused for his student ID, his t-shirt, a sneaker.

You send him away untouched as soon as the transaction

is complete and enjoy what provides you true satisfaction. Inflicting several scratches and a few bruises on your skin to serve as deceptive evidence of passion. Deciding how long you'll make me cower in a dark hotel room waiting for your call. Fantasizing about my fear that the call won't come. Growing aroused by my anxiety that I'll be abandoned without passport or money or memory. Climaxing with the certainty that without you I'm nothing, without you I'm lost. In the aftermath of your release, luxuriating in the truth that even if rescued by one agency or another from a dark hotel room, even restored to the identity of my first sixteen years, I would never recover from what has grown into two decades spent in your arms. Rehabilitation is not a possibility.

❖

Manuel Arroyo tried to concentrate on the new case file on his desk. The body of a strangled woman had been found in the river, near the site developed for Sevilla's 1992 World Exposition. People liked to say that the city wasn't the same since '92. In some ways, perhaps not. But the murder rate hadn't risen; incidents of violent crime weren't more numerous.

The case before Manuel appeared fairly routine. An act of domestic violence motivated by jealousy. The husband, who was the prime suspect, hadn't tried to flee the city. The evidence against him was already substantial and solid; whether Manuel uncovered further indications of his guilt or not, the man would be taken into custody shortly and almost certainly be arraigned for trial. The investigation

*promised to lead to a successful outcome, unlike that of the
Caballerizas murder.*

*In the past two weeks, Manuel had gone back to the
Trastamore once and Gimnasio Sevilla twice. He interviewed
the residents of the building for a final time. None of these
efforts produced results. The occupant of Bajo-E, the
apartment nearest the street door of Caballerizas, 4, again
asserted having been mistaken in thinking he noticed
something out of the ordinary around the time of the murder.
Maria del Carmen Vasquez still hadn't located the presumed
killer's passport information or a copy of his lease in her
files.*

*The Caballerizas case wasn't formally closed; the
investigation had been placed on inactive status until such
time as further information might surface. Manuel's current
directive was to wrap up an investigation of the woman found
murdered in the Guadalquiver as swiftly as possible. There
were hints within the homicide division that a review of the
detective's investigative procedures might be forthcoming
as a result of his lack of success with the Caballerizas case.
The relative freedom in which he had been allowed to work
in the past seemed in danger of being curtailed.*

*The failure of Olivier Ortega to surface added to the
sense of something having gone amiss in the most recent
investigation he had consulted on. Specific to this perception
was the fact that the pathologist hadn't submitted his report
on the Caballerizas murder before disappearing. It was a
startling oversight to be made by a man with a history of
being highly—some would say overly—conscientious in
carrying out his professional duties. Did Ortega ever make
a report on the Caballerizas case? Had he destroyed it prior*

to disappearing? Taken it with him, wherever he had gone? What might his reasons have been for doing so? At a time when he was already made to feel keenly aware of his failure to come up with answers, Manuel could supply none for these questions.

❖

A river of Spanish streams from the lips of the boy beneath my skin. For years he's waited for the day it might be safe for him to speak and for me to listen. He stumbles over sentences and trips over his tongue in haste to release words which have been dammed up for too long.

Está bien, I reassure him. *Ya lo sé. Te endiendo. No te preocupes más.* I want to cradle the boy in my arms. Rock away his worry, soothe him with a lullaby. He doesn't want my pity or consolation; he wants me to understand. His retreat down into the darkness was the result of fear at the first sight of your knives. He felt confused at realizing what you wanted to do with them. He knew he was unequipped to survive cutting blades, slicing razors. He was only a child. Just sixteen then; still sixteen now. For the past twenty years, he's thought he would die in darkness. He feared he would never again see light. *Lo comprendo todo,* I tell him. I understand everything. As though I too have moved into light after decades of darkness, I can see it all.

❖

I see you standing by the window in the moments before I venture out into the demanding night to find what you need.

From our apartment on the second floor, it's possible to see over the high wall of the monastery across the narrow street. The courtyards beyond are barely lit, as though only the illumination of faith is necessary to guide holy men toward their small stone cells. I don't ask what's wrong. I know why you suffer and how I can free you of pain.

For the past two weeks, while your torment has intensified, you've become increasingly distracted and on edge. You show little desire to share your body with me. Your interest in working out at the gym wanes; your appetite for meals I fix with special care during this difficult phase suffers. Shrugging off my touch, you go alone into the bedroom and sit on the edge of our bed. Your metal case clicks open as in vain you seek comfort from the stale souvenirs it contains. Your pain now is more acute than at any time before. It's more essential than ever that I find an effective remedy for what ails you.

I become aware of how agitated you must feel when you're driven to go out by yourself on the night before I'm scheduled to seek means for your solace. You rarely leave our apartment without me. You hate walking through the world without my presence at your side. The strain and exhaustion on your face whenever you return from a ten-day trip to secure funds for us shows how difficult it must be for you to survive without me for that long.

On this night, when you come back after several hours, you appear slightly less tense than before going out. You're sufficiently calm to be able to take care of details that require your attention on the following day. You register for the hotel room where I will go to wait for you that night. You begin the process of cleaning that will allow us to leave this city immediately after the specimen is finished with.

I dress in my hunting clothes amid air perfumed by ammonia and bleach and smoke. You're burning papers, scouring surfaces, wiping fingerprints from walls. Only a quick mopping up will be necessary when your experience has been completed. When I move toward the door, focused on my task at hand, I'm startled by a further indication that this moment is unlike any of the others to precede it. For the first time, you offer me advice on how I might go about finding what you need. Without turning from the window, not looking away from where believers chant and pray by candlelight, you break your silence.

"Why don't you try down by the river?" you suggest.

❖

Several times Raimunda almost asked Carmen Vasquez about what she knew of the occupant of Bajo-E. The real estate agent was frequently at Caballerizas, 4 to prepare 2-A for rental after the police finally unsealed it. Though claiming to be terribly busy, she always seemed to have time for café with Raimunda.

"I could get you a fortune for this place," she said, squinting at the widow's salon. "It would be understandable you might want to move after that mess next door." Apparently, Carmen had many interested tenants for 2-A prior to its official re-listing. The fact that few apartments ever became available in the neighbourhood overrode any unpleasant history attached to them. Carmen certainly wasn't advertising the reasons for 2-A's current vacancy. She knew she could count on Raimunda's discretion on this point. "If

the new tenants don't know in advance what happened next door, let's allow them to find out on their own, shall we?"she suggested.

Raimunda smiled. No, she wouldn't ask Carmen about Joaquin Bueso de Maderas, despite being confident that within ten minutes on the telephone, the real estate agent could discover his occupation, age, and D.N.I. number, as well as the amount of his rent. Raimunda would find out on her own.

Without turning on the exterior light, she felt her way down the stairs late that night. The marble surfaces of the outermost courtyard gleamed in the dark. No crack of light was visible beneath the closed door or between the closed shutters of the apartment to her left. The entire building seemed silent. Raimunda looked up toward the square of framed sky above and counted the stars it contained.

Her gaze was lowered by the sense that a point of light shone in the fountain before her. Stepping nearer to the pool, she heard something to her left. It was a man crying. Raimunda stiffened. No attempt seemed being made to stifle the sobs. As the widow listened to the sustained sound, she became convinced that it would continue until dawn. She took one step toward Bajo-E. She hesitated, shivering. The night contained the first hint of approaching winter. Raimunda turned and felt her way back upstairs in the dark.

❖

I flip open my cell phone to check that it's switched on and charged to receive your call. The hour and date illuminated by the device inadvertently catch my eye. I seem unable to perform a simple mathematical calculation that would tell me how much time has passed since I left you with the specimen. Thirty-six hours? Forty-eight?

My uncertainty strikes me as resembling the feeling I sometimes have on waking after having swallowed what was perhaps a particularly strong dose of bedtime tincture. On these occasions, I suspect several days or even a week might have passed since my eyes closed. The room looks different than the one in which I fell asleep. Could I have forgotten that we've moved into another apartment in another city? Maybe we've just arrived at a new site of operations following your recent experience with a specimen at the previous one. My cloudy mind would fumble at further questions.

Though we always sleep nude, I would find myself to be partly or fully dressed in clothes belonging neither to you nor to me. They don't quite fit. For a moment, I'm aware of the size of body that would be better contained by what I'm wearing. The clothes emit an alien scent that prickles my flesh and draws my attention to its surface. My skin signals that it holds souvenirs of ministrations I have no knowledge of receiving. Yet each occasion of my marking is etched as indelibly into my mind as upon my body.

These attentions for which I have no explanation would tend to appear not to have been paid with your knives and other usual instruments. Instead of sliced and cut, the flesh looks charred in some patches, eaten away in others. Is the strange scent of my clothes in fact one of smoke and acid lingering on my skin? As my mind weakly wonders, you enter the room naked. Your penis is partly erect. It swells and lengthens as you bend over me. You undress me, as though aroused less by the act of exposing by body than by fondling the clothes that cover it.

When you enter me, you're inside someone else. I'm aware that he's experiencing sensations that he's never felt before. *It won't hurt for long*, I wish to tell the boy as his whimpering emerges from my mouth. *Soon you'll get used to it and soon you'll live for it.* Awareness of his pain and fear detracts from my pleasure only for several strokes. When he's gone, I don't wonder where he went and why he left behind the clothes you removed from my body and dropped beside the bed. You're driving into me, you're driving away from him, you're driving out the unimportant questions of where I am and when this is.

Now, without your presence, I'm powerless to ward off wondering how long my exile from your arms has lasted. Thirty-six hours? Forty-eight? Numbers swim in my mind until they become washed away by wave after wave of vision which dissolves the mystery of how this hotel room can contain three items seemingly in possession of a boy who you make moan on the other side of the city.

Look.

I see you emerge from the black mouth of a tunnel beneath a bridge. On the riverbank before you, several members of a rowing club linger after their evening training. You approach the most beautiful of the boys, who stands slightly apart from the others. His dark hair is tousled by sweat. His deep chest still heaves from exercise. He's the one who waits with searching eyes.

You offer him a wad of *euros* to perform a fairly simple task. You give him replicas of the wrist brand and gold medallion you plan to stow in my athletic bag. For another hundred *euros,* you purchase his rowing club card. He's shown my photograph and instructed to wait for me in the vicinity on the following night. He should position himself within my radar and draw my attention. You explain several ways how this can be done.

After welcoming my approach and agreeing to go to my apartment, he must chatter with assumed excitement along the way. It's essential he make a point of fingering the braided band on his left wrist frequently, of touching the gold medallion around his neck often enough to draw my notice. His rowing club has to be mentioned. After I deliver him to you, and when he's promised that your instructions have been followed precisely, he'll receive a second payment equal to the one made in advance. Then he's free to go.

❖

Manuel shifted pages pertaining to his latest case, then stowed the closed file in a drawer of his desk. The suspect in the Guadalquiver murder had confessed to murdering his wife. Every detail of the man's statement was consistent with forensic evidence produced by the crime, as well as with the testimony of individuals associated with the couple. The concrete contents of the closed file made Manuel more keenly aware than ever that his investigation of the Caballerizas murder had been driven solely by supposition and presumption.

Neither forensic nor eyewitness evidence indicated that the victim had been killed by the second occupant of 2-A. The crime took place several days before the expiration of a lease for which no extension had been requested, according

*to Maria del Carmen Vasquez. Possibly the apartment
had been cleaned and personal belongings removed in
anticipation of vacating the premises. For one reason or
another, the other occupant left Sevilla in advance of the
victim, who encountered his killer then.*

*There was no evidence that the victim's earlier or more
recent mutilation had a direct connection to his murder. Or
that his companion was responsible for inflicting any of
the torture. Or that the relationship between the two men
had been sexual and/or romantic. Manuel looked upward,
as though his vision could penetrate the ceiling and see
deep into the famously blue Sevilla sky. He remembered
his involvement in cases seemingly as hopeless as this one,
which had ultimately been solved. He knew that the answer
to any question can fall out of empty air like the feather from
a wing of truth flying above.*

❖

Have my ostensible insights arrived with suspicious
clarity and speed? Does their occurrence constitute one more
manipulation on your part? Are my seeming revelations the
anticipated result of a meticulous set-up in the planning for
months? The gold chain, braided band, and rowing club
card were planted in my athletic bag with the conviction
that, unlike souvenirs provided for me to dispose of in the
past, these ones would undam a flood of confusion and
doubt. Your motive must be to discover whether my love
is strong enough to withstand any amount of uncertainty.
Whether it will survive this experience of being trapped in
a hotel room teeming with troubling questions. Although

the three clues I've been given might be of dubious value, they're all I have. I strain to decipher them. To see the truth hidden within them.

❖

Cafés and bars on either bank cast swaths of scarlet and blue and purple across a river. The black water renders the colours upon it more vivid and rich by contrast. Away from my boat, barely a ripple disturbs the surface. The evening is almost still. Flamenco carries from Triana *terrazas* with pristine clarity, with undiminished emotion. I'm rowing more powerfully than the other boys of the club; their boats are out of view, beyond the bend behind me.

Since my father left, I'm always first on the river and last to leave. I want to avoid listening to my mother cry in the kitchen. I want to remain away from rooms no longer filled with a rough, deep voice. My back and arms have become strong; one day they'll be able to row me all the way to Gran Canaria.

Each slice of my oars conjures cold, dark scent to rise with greater power from the water. It merges with warmer air above, fuses with aromas of garlic and olive oil from the cafés. At my stroke's ascendant point, several dozen drops of silver fall. I shoot beneath the bridge that crosses to Los Remedios. For a moment, I'm travelling through a danker element, amid greater darkness. Silver shards scattered by my oars shine more brightly. They hold the promise that one night I'll travel farther than to the Canary Islands. One night I'll row my boat among the stars. I'll steer between clusters of constellations. I'll float across the Milky Way.

❖

As though timed to intrude at just this moment, my cell erupts with a ringtone of sassy salsa. Before I can lift the phone to my ear, the song stops. No beep follows to indicate that voicemail has been left or a text sent. Only you have this number. It was keyed by your finger or, in error, by that of a stranger. If a call from you has been dropped, the cell will ring again in a moment. There's no point in my trying to call you. Your cell remains switched off until you finish with a specimen. Silence stretches. I'm aware the boy beneath my skin has stayed quiet for some time. He's leaving me undisturbed to understand what he's told me. He holds his breath in suspense. Will I be able to interpret his message from the darkness? Will I be able to find the answer that will lead us both to light?

❖

As the November nights turned cooler, Manuel felt unable to stay at home in the evening. His restless mood suggested he should call the woman he'd been seeing since shortly after his wife had left him. He usually went to spend a few days with Paula in Málaga once or perhaps twice a month. Seeming content with their long-standing arrangement, she never suggested it might be established on a firmer basis. She was nearly always available for him to visit, but didn't give the impression of waiting for his call. Manuel understood that she didn't see other men, for reasons having nothing to do with him.

Paula owned a small hotel which had been in her family for years, but she lived in an apartment on the other side of the city. A good deal of her time was spent socializing with members of the local artistic circle, Manuel gathered. She mentioned that she often read through the night. She didn't offer to introduce Manuel to her friends, and he didn't ask about the volumes of French literary theory and German philosophy scattered through her rooms.

When on occasion they discussed a case on which Manuel was working, her insights wouldn't be useful in practical terms, but were always startling. The detective felt no inclination to talk to Paula about the Caballerizas murder. Despite his restlessness, it didn't seem right to leave Sevilla even for a few days now. Unfinished business remained for him here and required his continued presence. That was what drew him out into the streets at night.

He wandered past the cafés and bars along the river. Sometimes he crossed Puente Isabel II over to Triana or made his way up to the Alameda. Invariably, he would realize that a roundabout route had managed to bring him to Menendez Pelayo. As the nights turned cold, fewer men passed beneath the orange trees along the avenue toward the Trastamore.

Standing in front of Olivier Ortega's building, Manuel felt conspicuous, exposed. He looked up at the windows in the southern corner of the third storey. They were always unlit. The detective sometimes suspected he could see a figure moving in the darkness beyond the glass. It was only a trick of the light, he knew. Only a sleight of his mind. A similar psychological ruse, realized Manuel, led him to believe that the key to the case whose unresolved nature urged him night after night out into the street had vanished with Olivier Ortega.

❖

If the boy I found beside the river was playing a role, his performance was almost flawless. It did strike me at the time that I discovered him almost too easily, too quickly. Like an offering of the god of darkness, he drifted into my field of vision, near the opening of the tunnel beneath the bridge, as I approached the embankment.

Anxious for the second half of your promised payment, he made a point of catching my attention before I could consider other possibilities. With what I thought endearing ostentation, he stretched to reveal the clotted muscles of his back, the wings of wide shoulders. We exchanged only several words before he began walking away from the river with me. Fingering his red and blue wrist band, touching his gold medallion, talking about the rowing club: all according to script.

His nervousness was probably genuine, though due to anxiety over *euros* rather than to excitement at the prospect of a sexual experience. He made just one slip: the mention of being abandoned by his father. I can't see how that detail could fit into your scenario. Replayed in my mind, the comment seems made in a tone distinct from the rest of the boy's chatter. The boy blurted the words without intending. They emerged accidentally. Why? Does the fact have such importance for him that it insists on being spoken whether he wants it to be or not? Whatever the reason for its utterance, the skimpy phrase appears to be the single true clue among all those planted with the aim of deception.

❖

My father stands in the doorway of my bedroom in the middle of the night. On the table in the kitchen behind him rests a scrap of paper containing the words *Gone to Gran Canaria.* Next to the note lies a receipt acknowledging payment for five years of future dues for the rowing club I've recently joined. Breeze carrying the scent of geraniums enters the open French doors of my bedroom; it scarcely stirs the white curtains over the open windows. My father unfastens a fine gold chain holding a gold medallion from around his neck. He drops it at the foot of my bed. The sound of the medallion and chain landing on tile is too faint to wake me.

❖

My eyes are opened by bright light. I'm still in the hotel room. Did I succumb to forbidden sleep and indulge in unauthorized dreams? An unconscious mind is powerless to resist thought which wakefulness can guard against.

It's to prevent the occurrence of this phenomenon that you hold the glass of clouded liquid to my lips after our bodies have shuddered and spilled at night. I swallow obediently. The tincture's bitter taste resembles that of the saliva and semen already haunting my mouth. I fall asleep thirty minutes later and waken eight hours afterward with the sense no time has passed. Even fleeting dreams haven't had a chance to flit through my drugged mind.

I appreciate your assistance in enabling me to sleep undisturbed because it saves me from feeling that in the darkness I travel far away from you to find myself lost in lonely lands. Any dreams I remembered on waking would resemble nightmares, I suspect. Intuition warns me of the frightening shape those images would take.

A nude body lies face down on a bed. The boy is bound and gagged. Some of the blood on the heavily stained sheets appears to have been caused by multiple stab wounds to the boy's skin. Three knives of varying sizes, whose blades seem designed for distinct purposes, rest near the body in a way that makes me think they've been carelessly discarded there. I can feel the weight and shape each knife would have in my hand, how all of them would fit my grip exactly.

The remainder of the blood is obviously the result of trauma inflicted by objects resembling oversized nails or screws, which have been inserted into the body. The largest protrudes from the boy's rectum. I concentrate on counting the number of punctures visible on the body to avoid listening to the sound it makes. The moaning might be an expression of pleasure; it's uttered too weakly to allow for a clear interpretation. When the sound stops, I realize I'll never know what emotion inspired it.

A sense that my chance has been lost to understand one facet of the truth propels me to seize the opportunity to comprehend what remains. I take one step forward. I reach down to turn over the body. It's surprising how cold the boy's flesh is. I'm puzzled at how heavy his body is. Only my desire to see the hidden face empowers me to turn the body over.

The action seems to require enormous effort, as though I were shifting a submerged dead weight through a medium as resistant as water. As he is turned over with infinite slowness, I feel myself rising above the sunken boy until no point of contact remains between him and me. A process leading toward revelation has been set in motion. It requires no further assistance on my part to be completed. I ascend higher and higher, until I'm looking down through quantums of darkness. Both the night and the water below possess a clarity that should allow vision to penetrate their depths, yet I'm barely able to discern the blunt shape far beneath me. I can't see the face I want to see. My eyes are dazzled by stars that bob in the night through which I float.

Look closer.

Despite the hotel room's brightness, I can't see the face I long to see. I search the space in hopes of discovering the switch for a stronger light and come to rest on the television in the corner. I'm tempted to turn it on. I suddenly feel curious to know what's happening in the world now and what changes might have taken place on this planet during the past twenty years. Have new nations been formed and new species emerged? When I reach to pick up the remote, I find that my left hand has been holding the rowing club card. It was apparently removed from my back pocket and placed in my grip while I slept. I ignore the lure of images from the outside world and inspect the one in my hand again. Is this face in the card's photo the face I long to see? I look more closely at the information printed below the photo. Name: Jose Manuel. Place and year of birth: Sevilla, 1975. Date of membership issue: 08 March, 1990. Lilting laughter lifts my eyes from the data that confronts them. I glance around the room in search of the source of the voice. One corner is pooled with shadow, though no object lies between it and the light.

My cell erupts again with salsa. Bar after bar of jaunty music plays. You're calling to tell me you're on your way to me. You've finished extracting pleasure from the current specimen or from my painful, prolonged wait for you. It doesn't matter which. For the first time, I don't answer your call. The music stops. After a moment, it resumes. I switch off my cell. Now you're the one waiting in uncertainty. You're wondering if you've left me alone one too many times. Despite the state of helplessness in which with scientific precision I've been placed, have I dared to seek escape from your reach? Are you already hurrying toward this hotel in hope that I'll still be here, in fear that I've already left?

Look closer. See farther. Understand more.

Encouraged by the voice from the corner of the room, I squint at the rowing club card. A bent and slightly stained condition supports an age equal to the date printed on it. The red and blue threads of the *pulsera* on my left wrist appear faded with time. The gold of the medallion at my throat is tarnished. You didn't buy the three items several days ago. They've been locked inside your metal case for twenty years.

These souvenirs of the night I was found beside a river have been kept in readiness for when they would finally be needed. You planted them in my athletic bag not in order to make me doubt your love but to serve as final proof of it. The power contained in these items would encourage the boy beneath my skin to speak and enable me to hear his words. They would unearth memory, unlock vision, invite dreams.

You knew what would happen. I would turn on light, turn off my cell. I would set myself free. Haven't you always lacked the strength to let go of tokens of your experiences with the gifts I've offered you? Haven't you always depended on me to release you from those mementos of the past? Aren't you now counting on me to gather the courage to free both you and me?

❖

One day Esperanza wasn't sitting in her chair on the sidewalk. The dim room down the six steps was empty. Something bad had happened after I walked away from Esperanza with my new blue and red band the previous afternoon. I didn't know what; my mother wouldn't say. In a lowered voice, she spoke with other women who had gathered like anxious pigeons at the end of the block.

Later I learned that a man followed Esperanza into the cellar when she went down there for a moment. No one saw him go in or come out. Noticing the abandoned tray of coloured string on the sidewalk chair, a neighbour descended six steps to see what might be wrong. Selena took her sister away that night.

"The poor thing," my mother murmured to my father, sautéing bread in olive oil and garlic for his *cena* at ten o'clock. "It would have been better for her and the sister if she hadn't lived." For a long time, the world seemed a darker place, as though a sifting of black covered its colours. I would touch the blue and red band around my left wrist. It felt smooth and rough at once. Esperanza had braided the strings so tightly they would never loosen, never fray. I could feel my red blood pulse a repeated promise through the blue vein beneath the band.

❖

I will free both of us. I glance toward the shadow that in the corner is becoming solid. You too, I promise. And also Esperanza. First let me look one last time at the substance that I must escape from to spark liberation for us all. I undress beneath the glaring bathroom light and in the mirror look at the body you've always discouraged me from inspecting closely.

It's been easy to obey your wish. Having little desire to study my incorrectly marked flesh, I am able to disregard the sight of it while in the shower or in bed. Attention is to be paid only to my face; its skin must be scrupulously tended with a regimen of expensive serums and creams and lotions. My sense has been that just the most recent scars appear unsightly and that ones acquired earlier are faded to the point of near invisibility. I've imagined the marks are almost melted away by the balm of your lips.

Only now do I realize why our curtains stay closed and why our rooms are usually lit by glowing candles and soft lamps. It's understandable that the skin reflected in the mirror before me should never be seen under bright light. Except for my face and neck and hands, I'm covered completely with scars which appear to be layered one on top of the other to form an unbroken surface of rough scales. This might be the thick hide of a species of reptile that has become extinct or has yet to emerge on earth.

The contrast between the smoothness of my face and the rest of my skin alternately suggests the result of a scientific experiment gone grotesquely wrong. I look quickly away from several areas of my body which seem to have been mutilated as well as marked. That you're able to touch me even occasionally, brutally, serves as undeniable proof of your extraordinary love. It's equally evident that no eyes but yours deserve to be confronted with the sickening sight to face me now. Most importantly, I must protect the whistler of the brave, jaunty tune in the other room from witnessing what the mirror reveals. It's bad enough he's aware of what has happened to the surface beneath which he's hidden. Putting my shirt back on, I take special care to roll the sleeves down to my wrists.

"Jose Manuel," I say to the boy waiting for me to emerge from the bathroom. "This belongs to you." While he studies the rowing club card, I observe that twenty years spent in darkness haven't damaged him. He looks exactly as he did on being found beside a river at sixteen. His eyes are clear and bright in an unlined face. His back is broad and strong; his legs are straight and long. The clothes whose disturbing aroma compelled me to take them off fit him perfectly.

The scent of the material has been intensified by contact with the boy's skin. No longer unsettling to me, now purely beautiful, wave after wave of something clean and cold mixed with something rich and dark emits from him. I glance away as the boy stows the card in his back pocket. My sight has seized enough of a vision to sustain me to the end. If I look any longer, I'll never be able to stop. I won't be able to let him go. I can see out of the corner of my eye that he's more frightened by this moment than I am.

Although we've lived together on the most intimate terms for twenty years, we're shy with each other now. We're not used to being separate. To break a strained silence,

I remove the blue and red *pulsera* from my left wrist and place it around his. Two or three or four days without sleep and food must have left me more exhausted than I feel. My fingers fumble to tie the braided band for him. My hands shake as I try to unfasten the fine gold chain from around my neck and from behind secure it around his.

Still unaccustomed to bright light, my eyes are watering and I can scarcely see. I can barely resist touching my lips just once to the swath of naked nape an inch away. He would turn and fold himself within my arms. He's holding his breath in suspense. Then his back swells with an inhalation of air.

"There," I say, wiping my eyes before he can see them. "You're ready. It's time to go. It's now or never. But wait just a moment. First I must ask you to do one thing for me. It's the only thing I'll ask and the last thing I'll ask."

Listen.

The man behind the registration desk looks startled when the boy and I pass through the lobby of the hotel.

"Checking out?" he calls as we reach the entrance and step out into the street. The early evening air is warm, and the sidewalks are crowded with shoppers. We walk quickly. I can tell the boy beside me is anxious and eager at once. For reassurance, he fingers the band of red and blue around his wrist, touches the gold medallion resting just beneath his throat. He chatters nervously about how much he's looking forward to rowing on the river again. Barely listening to his words, savouring the sound of his voice, I provide rote responses to put him at ease. The empty athletic bag hangs from my shoulder; from force of habit, I'm leaving no evidence behind in the hotel room.

Street lights switch on as we pass through the Plaza de la Encarnación. Octagons of glass attached to the stone walls of the passage beyond offer a guiding glow. My heart begins to bang like a fist. I pray the boy will be able to keep the promise I made him give before leaving the hotel. When we reach the second plaza, I told him, he must turn left while I continue forward. Like two strangers who, for a time, have shared the same journey due to a coincidence of time and space, no goodbye will be necessary when separate destinations assert themselves, and we go our own ways.

The Plaza de la Passión de Jesus appears ahead. The boy at my side is looking at me, I know. He's hoping I'll turn and say there's no need for us to separate after all. I keep my eyes fixed forward.

"Please trust me and please believe me," I asked him in the hotel. "One day you'll see it's for the best." We cross the square and arrive at the street I told him to turn down. He breathes quickly, as though pulling oars with all his strength through resistant water. His step falters. Then he turns left while I continue forward. The scent of something cold and clean mixed with something rich and dark grows faint, soon dissolves.

Don't look back, I warned him. Keep moving forward. In ten minutes, you'll reach La Macarena. The old barrio of crumbling churches hasn't changed very much in twenty years. It will be easy for you to find your way through the twisting streets and make your way back home. Your mother is waiting for you in her kitchen in the Calle Pozo. The crippled man still repairs guitars in his shop on the ground floor of the building. Red and blue ribbons still splash colour on the white walls of your bedroom. Geraniums still bloom on the balcony across the narrow street from your window.

Don't look back, I caution myself. The empty athletic bag weighs heavily from my shoulder as though filled with stones. The glowing lamps seem to be leading away, not beckoning forward. I enter the Plaza de la Alfalfa. Starlings are screaming as shrilly in the plane trees as the children in their playground. Without glancing, I move past the area enclosed by low red slats in one corner of the square. I continue steadily forward into the labyrinth beyond.

An immense church, dark and locked, rises in front of me. Pausing before the adjacent building, I sense the monastery to my back across the narrow street. One of two large keys unlocks a wooden door studded with brass; a switch illuminates the patio inside. Across a gleaming marble floor, past potted ferns and palms, beyond columns and arches, a further patio beckons. In the centre of this one stands a still fountain.

Rain must have fallen during the past few days. The fountain basin contains an inch of water, reflections of pale blue stars. Patterns of Pisces, arrangements of Aries. Hearing a sound from the apartment to my right, I become aware the patio light is buzzing loudly, insistently. I climb the stairs to the second floor and with a second key unlock a door. The space beyond is dimly lit with candles, and heavy with a scent of wax. In the bedroom waits a man I don't recognize at once. I wonder whether I've unlocked the wrong door in the wrong building. Then I realize this seeming stranger must be you.

You look exhausted and sick; you look strained and sad. Two or three or four nights ago, I might have brought you phantom flesh and left you to suffer alone with thwarted desire. While waiting for my return, you haven't eaten or slept or bathed. I hope you'll have the strength to love me one last time. I pray you'll be able to set both of us free.

I must make it as easy for you as possible. Setting down the athletic bag, I quickly undress. Sight of my mutilated body makes you inhale sharply. I lie on the bed without glancing at the knives and other instruments that wait on the sheets. The relative sharpness of blades doesn't matter now; the varying length and girth of steel rods has become unimportant. *Please trust me and please believe me*, I want to urge you. *One day you'll understand it's for the best.* You bend over me, and for a moment, I look into your beautiful eyes. Then I stare at a candle burning on a dresser across the room. The flame is as golden as the lamps that are leading a boy home.

His step quickens as he nears Calle Pozo. He runs lightly up the stairs. Soon I smell the warm, rich scent of olive oil and garlic. His mother must be sautéing bread for him. Perhaps tonight there'll be a slice of fragrant ham.

It must be several hours since you started work with your knives because you're breathing heavily, as though from long and physically demanding labour. From time to time, I sense, you stop to rest until you re-gather strength. The candle has burned more than halfway down.

There's no hurry, I'd reassure you if I hadn't moved beyond language now. *Be patient*, I would like to tell the sixteen-year-old boy standing on his bedroom balcony. There's plenty of time for him to row on a river, to drift in his boat amid the cerulean stars. For several years, he'll be unable to sleep without a light burning in the next room, and small spaces will make him anxious. For more than several years, he'll be apprehensive of men, frightened of what they might want to do to him.

Don't worry, I wish I could tell him. *It doesn't matter whether your father returns from Gran Canaria or from any other island that tempted him away. One day, I promise, you'll be found by a man whose shoulders are wider and whose back is stronger than those of your father and those of mine. He will love you completely, and he'll never leave as long as you love him completely in return.*

The candle has nearly gone out. Its light will last only several minutes more.

Don't stop, I want to encourage you. *You're almost finished, my lungs have breathed almost a million breaths. We're nearly free.*

When the freed boy gazes into the mirror, he'll sometimes see an image that seems doubly exposed. My features waver beneath his, as though under an inch of water. When his face lines with age, after its features settle, only a single reflection will look back at him. His. Mine. Ours. Now and then, influenced by memory of its years spent beating in time with mine, his heart will play at a tempo faster or slower than his pulse.

My heart is bursting with happiness. It joyously explodes me into the stars as the candle burns out and bells chime in celebration at the top of the church next door.

The chanting of prayers carries from a dozen small stone cells across the street. The sound drowns out your sobbing. It travels across the city and reaches a boy on a balcony. His face turns in the direction of distant bells and prayers. Through the darkness before him drifts a feather from the wing of a bird wakened by appeals from God to ascend into the dark blue night. The far-off sound fades to be replaced by music of a guitar being strummed below the balcony. A crippled man is testing the instrument he's spent the day repairing. Again and again the tune breaks off at the moment just before the boy listening above can decide whether it's plaintive or playful.

PART FOUR

The owner of the Hotel Zahira leafed through his registration book in search of an entry made several weeks ago for number 302. The room's most recent guest had remarked that it seemed to contain quite a strong aroma. The scent wasn't disagreeable, she had taken pains to add. She didn't wish to convey that it had interfered with a very pleasant stay in a very pleasant hotel.

For Carlos Montoya, a slight suggestion that anything might be amiss with his establishment was cause for concern. Apologizing to the guest, he discounted her bill by ten percent and immediately went to investigate the room in question. A moment later, he called the chambermaid to join him there. She agreed 302 did possess a definite aroma. She'd noticed something for the past three weeks or so, though the space had been cleaned to her usual high standards after each of its occupancies during that time.

The hotel owner didn't doubt this. The woman had performed scrupulously for him for years. Yet the room was certainly haunted by a scent. Carlos couldn't place a name to it. Something dark and cold mixed with something warm *and rich? He asked the chambermaid to do him the favour of cleaning the room again and leave the windows open to air it out, then he returned to the hotel lobby. An hour later, his employee reported she had been unable to locate a possible source for the scent while cleaning the room again.*

Carlos thanked her. He would leave 302 unoccupied for several days. As the chambermaid moved away to resume work, Carlos began leafing through the registration book. He had little doubt which recent guest of 302 had left troubling traces behind. The smoothness with which the Hotel Zahira operated, combined with the quality of client it attracted, made the kind of incident connected to this visitor's stay both rare and memorable. The man had occupied the room alone, though Carlos was under the impression that a second man, who registered for it with him, would be joining him. This didn't happen.

What occurred instead was that, two days into an occupancy which had been peaceful until then, another guest on the third floor informed the assistant manager on duty at the time of a disturbance in 302. Given the nature of the matter and his relative inexperience, Pablo had been quite right to call Carlos to help deal with it. The two of them went up to the third floor. From the room in question, the sound of a man crying carried clearly out into the hallway. It was obviously an expression of distress or pain.

Becoming quite agitated by the sound, Pablo wished to knock on the door of 302 and ask if the man inside needed help of some kind. Carlos firmly overruled his assistant. It was the policy of the Hotel Zahira to respect the privacy of its guests. While the management was prepared do everything possible to ensure clients' comfort, it would be presumptuous to offer services that hadn't been sought. As though to confirm the correctness of this stance, the sound of crying in 302 abruptly ceased in the midst of Carlos's explanation.

The two men returned to the lobby. Pablo was instructed to keep a close eye on 302 and to call his employer again if the situation demanded it. Fortunately, nothing further untoward arose in relation to the guest in question, although his departure two days later was somewhat puzzling. He appeared in the lobby not with the man who was presumably to have joined him at the hotel, but with a boy who, in age and resemblance, might have been his own son.

This boy hadn't been seen going up to 302 nor, remarkably, was it noticed that the occupant had left the room even once during his four-day stay. Carrying the athletic bag that comprised his sole luggage, the guest moved quickly with his companion toward the street door. He didn't respond when Carlos called to ask whether he was checking out. This inquiry was made in part because a ten-night stay in the room had been paid for with cash in advance.

The owner of the Hotel Zahira gave up leafing through his registration book. What did it matter? If he began puzzling over the behaviour of even his most pleasant guests, there'd be no end to it. He shook his head in dismissal. The gesture was insufficiently powerful to banish the scent that had trailed after the departing guest three weeks before and that would, Carlos Montoya suspected, linger in Room 302 indefinitely.

❖

"My professionalism has always been beyond reproach," Maria del Carmen Vasquez declared once again to her companion. Of late, she and Raimunda Nuñez de Guerra Moreno had taken to meeting for an occasional aperitif in the Plaza de la Alfalfa, although they had little in common besides their respective stakes in Caballerizas, 4.

Carmen's interest in nurturing the relationship was motivated by her sustained wish to acquire the other woman's apartment for her agency one way or another, suspected Raimunda. The widow drew her fur coat more closely around her shoulders. The December evenings had grown chilly. The plane trees at the edge of the square were bare of leaves and fewer children played in the enclosed area in one corner. It might have been more comfortable to sit over a fino inside, but the smoke from the real estate agent's numerous cigarettes made Raimunda nauseous.

As usual, she chose not to respond to her companion's outburst tonight. The real estate agent remained offended by aspersions cast on her agency by various discoveries made during the course of the investigation of the unfortunate incident in 2-A. Her failure to produce records which contained passport and other legally required information pertaining to the recent tenant of that apartment had been reported to the Sevilla Housing Authority.

It had further come to light that not only did Carmen charge the equivalent of two months' rent as a security deposit when only one is permitted, but only half that sum made its way into the bank account of 2-A's owner where, improperly levied or not, it belonged. As a consequence of these irregularities, the Inmobiliaria Boteros had been fined a considerable sum.

While the amount of the penalty didn't seriously affect her balance sheet, Carmen continued to feel offended by this insinuation that her agency was a fly-by-night operation that preyed on vulnerable individuals. She still placed blame for the 2-A fiasco on her former assistant.

"Time after time I've believed I was mentoring a protégé only to discover I was feeding a shark," she bitterly complained. "I've had it with ambitious blonde señoritas. From now on, I'm hiring only dark-eyed boys who may be incapable of sending an email but who know very well how to smile charmingly."

Waving away cigarette smoke, Raimunda changed the topic. She confided that she found the new occupants of 2-A enchanting. He was a rising young architect with one of the top firms in the city, and she was the modern type of woman who chooses to stay in the home when she could easily pursue a brilliant career outside. The two little tots were adorable. Raimunda had been right to ignore her daughter's advice to move from Caballerizas, 4 in the aftermath of the unpleasantness next door. The more recent incident to have occurred in the building, down in Bajo-E, really hadn't affected her at all. "I've never eaten or slept better in my life," Raimunda said, stroking her sable with satisfaction. Her impeccable appearance fortified this claim.

❖

The suicide in Bajo-E wasn't discovered as quickly as the murder in 2-A had been. Two days after the cleaning girl noticed an unpleasant odour emitting from the silent, shuttered apartment off the outermost courtyard, the

Presidente of the building's Communidad, who lived up in 1-B, called the police.

Manuel Arroyo was given a copy of the letter found with the body—not because he would be investigating the suicide, but because the document was addressed to him and related to the murder that had taken place six weeks earlier in the building. In the letter, composed in a miniscule handwriting that was difficult to read, Joaquin Polo Bueso apologized for not having been more forthcoming while interviewed about the event in 2-A.

The crime had occurred at a time of great distress for him. The nature of his crisis wasn't directly related to the murder and bore no significance in what little he had to say about it. However, it was due to the sleeplessness he suffered during this period that, three or four nights before the crime, he saw the victim enter the building and then leave several minutes later. In both instances, which must have taken place well after midnight, the man was alone.

Joaquin was struck that the man was in a highly agitated state which resembled his own. It was this sense of seeing his distress embodied by another which made the moment remarkable. That the sighting took place just when he believed he could no longer bear an unbearable burden, when he'd given up hope of receiving relief from his torment, added to its extraordinary impact.

During the following days, he felt as though his pain had been taken from him. A relative stranger, someone he'd never spoken to, was shouldering it for him.

Salvation is possible. Grace can be received.

The next time Joaquin saw the man enter the building, on the evening before his death, it seemed apparent that he was suffering from having absorbed another's anguish. Learning of his murder so soon afterward, he felt responsible for it. The death hadn't been inflicted by a sharp knife; it was caused by the crushing weight of a double burden. Now that full weight fell on Joaquin. He could barely breathe beneath it. He could scarcely speak while being interviewed by Manuel Arroyo. Only now could he share what he knew to be the truth. Another human being had died for him. Now he would give his life for a fellow sufferer. Perhaps for Manuel Arroyo.

❖

Manuel added the suicide's letter to his file for the Caballerizas case, though it didn't really alter what was there. The investigation remained dormant. Manuel had a hunch that while this murder would remain unsolved, its implications would continue to reach out to him whether he wanted them to or not. He suspected he would always feel that a second detective, nameless and unknown, was pursuing the case.

This invisible agent would shadow him as persistently as he would a prime suspect. In Manuel's path would be planted clues which didn't clarify a mystery but only served to insist that answers would always remain tantalizingly out of reach.

The whereabouts of Olivier Ortega continued to be an unsolved secret. The man still hadn't been in contact with the Sevilla Homicide Division or with any of the other professional bodies he was locally associated with. One day, Manuel called Maria del Carmen Vasquez to ask her to find out the status of Ortega's apartment through her sources. The real estate agent called back twenty minutes later.

After reporting that six months' future rent had been paid by the occupant of Menendez Pelayo prior to his disappearance, she inquired: "Made any more calls to the Housing Authority lately?" His caller curtly disconnected before Manuel could ask what she meant. Instead of wondering about what suddenly seemed like one too many obscurities, the detective entered a Málaga number on his cell. He had more unpaid leave banked up than he could ever use. He would see whether Paula was free for him to visit and whether this time she'd like him to stay for more than a few days. The only mystery he was interested in exploring now lay within a woman's arms.

Following his return to Sevilla from a ten-day visit in Málaga, Manuel Arroyo received a postcard from Ibiza. It was the first to arrive for him from the island since the one sent by his son fifteen years before. The card presented a colour scene of a Mediterranean sunset. As though there was risk of the banal image being misinterpreted, a small-font caption on the other side explained, in four languages, that it showed "Sunset at Playa de la Corona." The message on the card had been printed in neat capital letters: "Everything will be all right."

No salutation preceded these words, nor was a signature attached to them. Manuel was initially annoyed by the author's attempt at anonymity. Did Olivier Ortega imagine his identity wouldn't immediately be fathomed? Why would he suppose it was necessary to communicate under a veil of secrecy? Manuel quickly came to believe the opposite might be true. A signature was superfluous because Ortega had absolute confidence that its recipient would have no doubt who sent the card. Did he have similar faith Manuel would be able to understand his message?

The brief phrase became increasingly cryptic to the detective during the following days. It seemed to present different implications according to his particular mood. Sometimes the words possessed the quality of a prophecy or of a promise; at others, they might have been offered in the spirit of reassurance, in an effort to provide comfort.

Was Ortega suggesting the present needed his guarantee that one day it would be less painful and difficult? For whom? For Manuel Arroyo? For Olivier Ortega? For everyone? After carrying the postcard around in his pocket for a week, Manuel placed it, alongside the pair sent by his son, in the album that also contained photographs of the missing boy. Physical proximity seemed to dissolve differences between the messages of the three cards and between the identities of their two authors.

Eventually there remained a single message spoken by a single voice. Especially at sunset, when the river was briefly transformed into a path of flecked gold, Manuel heard his son's promise that everything would be all right.

About the Author

Patrick Roscoe is the author of eight books of fiction, including the novels *The Lost Oasis* and *God's Peculiar Care*. His widely published and anthologized fiction has won two CBC Literary Awards, two Western Magazine Awards, a National Magazine Award, the *Canadian Fiction Magazine* Annual Contributors Prize, the Lorian Hemingway Short Story Award, a *Prairie Fire* Short Fiction Competition Prize, and a *Prism International* Short Fiction Competition Prize; it has also received a pair of Distinguished Story citations from *Best American Stories*, and is frequently included in *Best Canadian Stories*.

Books Available From Bold Strokes Books

Fool's Gold by Jess Faraday.1895. Overworked secretary Ira Adler thinks a trip to America will be relaxing. But rattlesnakes, train robbers, and the U.S. Marshals Service have other ideas. (978-1-62639-340-0)

The Indivisible Heart by Patrick Roscoe. An investigation into a gruesome psycho-sexual murder and an account of the victim's final days are interwoven in this dark detective story of the human heart. (978-1-62639-341-7)

Big Hair and a Little Honey by Russ Gregory. Boyfriend troubles abound as Willa and Grandmother land new ones and Greg tries to hold on to Matt while chasing down a shipment of stolen hair extensions. (978-1-62639-331-8)

Death by Sin by Lyle Blake Smythers. Two supernatural private detectives in Washington, D.C., battle a psychotic supervillain spreading a new sex drug that only works on gay men, increasing the male orgasm and killing them. (978-1-62639-332-5)

Buddha's Bad Boys by Alan Chin. Six stories, six gay men trudging down the road to enlightenment. What they each find is the last thing in the world they expected. (978-1-62639-244-1)

Play It Forward by Frederick Smith. When the worlds of a community activist and a pro basketball player collide, little do they know that their dirty little secrets can lead to a public scandal...and an unexpected love affair. (978-1-62639-235-9)

GingerDead Man by Logan Zachary. Paavo Wolfe sells horror but isn't prepared for what he finds in the oven or the bathhouse; he's in hot water again, and the killer is turning up the heat. (978-1-62639-236-6)

Myth and Magic: Queer Fairy Tales, edited by Radclyffe and Stacia Seaman. Myth, magic, and monsters—the stuff of childhood dreams (or nightmares) and adult fantasies. (978-1-62639-225-0)

Balls & Chain by Eric Andrews-Katz. In protest of the marriage equality bill, the son of Florida's governor has been kidnapped. Agent Buck 98 is back, and the alligators aren't the only things biting. (978-1-62639-218-2)

Blackthorn by Simon Hawk. Rian Blackthorn, Master of the Hall of Swords, vowed he would not give in to the advances of Prince Corin, but he finds himself dueling with more than swords as Corin pursues him with determined passion. (978-1-62639-226-7)

Café Eisenhower by Richard Natale. A grieving young man who travels to Eastern Europe to claim an inheritance finds friendship, romance, and betrayal, as well as a moving document relating a secret lifelong love affair. (978-1-62639-217-5)

Murder in the Arts District by Greg Herren. An investigation into a new and possibly shady art gallery in New Orleans' fabled Arts District soon leads Chanse into a dangerous world of forgery, theft…and murder. A Chanse MacLeod mystery. (978-1-62639-206-9)

Rise of the Thing Down Below by Daniel W. Kelly. Nothing kills sex on the beach like a fishman out of water…Third in the Comfort Cove Series. (978-1-62639-207-6)

Calvin's Head by David Swatling. Jason Dekker and his dog, Calvin, are homeless in Amsterdam when they stumble on the victim of a grisly murder—and become targets for the calculating killer, Gadget. (978-1-62639-193-2)

The Return of Jake Slater by Zavo. Jake Slater mistakenly believes his lover, Ben Masters, is dead. Now a wanted man in Abilene, Jake rides to Mexico to begin a new life and heal his broken heart. (978-1-62639-194-9)

The Thief Taker by William Holden. Unreliable lovers, twisted family secrets, and too many dead bodies wait for Thomas Newton in London—where he soon discovers that all the plotting is aimed directly at him. (978-1-62639-054-6)

Waiting for the Violins by Justine Saracen. After surviving Dunkirk, a scarred and embittered British nurse returns to Nazi-occupied Brussels to join the Resistance, and finds that nothing is fair in love and war. (978-1-62639-046-1)

Turnbull House by Jess Faraday. London 1891: Reformed criminal Ira Adler has a new, respectable life—but will an old flame and the promise of riches tempt him back to London's dark side…and his own? (978-1-60282-987-9)

Stronger Than This by David-Matthew Barnes. A gay man and a lesbian form a beautiful friendship out of grief when their soul mates are tragically killed. (978-1-60282-988-6)

Death Came Calling by Donald Webb. When private investigator Katsuro Tanaka is hired to look into the death of a high profile lawyer, he becomes embroiled in a case of murder and mayhem. (978-1-60282-979-4)

Lightning Source UK Ltd.
Milton Keynes UK
UKHW04f0658280818
327907UK00001B/79/P